Wolf Moon

By

J.E. Taylor

J.E. TAYLOR
SUPERNATURAL SUSPENSE
& DARK FANTASY AUTHOR

Wolf Moon

Alessandra and Hunter have a price on their heads. Can they escape their fate, or will the sins of the past lead them to their death?

In the eyes of the werewolf council, Alessandra Tate and Hunter Blaez committed the ultimate sin. Humans were killed at the hands of a werewolf, and the price for taking a human life is death.

After being on the run for three months, Alessandra's nightmares are still plagued with the acts of that evening. Never again will she trust a man to get close enough to betray her, even Hunter Blaez, her beta wolf and protector.

Hunter has other ideas. He has been in love with Alessandra for years, but all she ever saw was her second in command. Even rescuing her from certain death and following her into damnation wasn't enough for her to see him as a man.

When the council catches Hunter, Alessandra must choose between surviving without him, or risking her life to save the only man she truly loves.

Preface

"HEY ALLY, WANT TO come up and party?"

His casual invitation interrupted her stride. Alessandra looked up from the sidewalk, hugging her books. Frat house boys ogled her from the balcony. At least twice a day since the semester started, she heard the catcall, but so had every other sorority girl on the block who walked by the Alpha Beta Pi house.

Jeremy leaned against the railing with a beer in his hand, smiling down at her, his bright green eyes reminding her of a wild mountain lion, and she suppressed a shiver. He raised his beer and, with a slight tilt of his head, said, "Come on, Ally. We won't bite."

His smooth voice caressed her ears, and she paused, inhaling deeply and memorizing his musky scent.

Yeah, but I might.

"Why should I?" Alessandra turned fully toward the house, flipping her long black hair over her shoulder and placing her hand on her hip, waiting for an answer.

He drained his beer and put his index finger up before he disappeared. Stepping out the front door moments later, he trotted down the sidewalk, stopping a few feet in front of her. "Come party with me." His gaze drifted over her in that hungry come-hither expression, matching the seductive tone in his voice.

She batted her eyelashes and tilted her head to the right, studying his cocky sureness. His reputation of slam, bam, thank you ma'am, the equivalent of a male whore ran through her head, and now his sights were set on her. "Again, why should I?" Alessandra asked, toying with him.

"Because I've wanted you since I first set eyes on you." Jeremy leaned in as he spoke, his breath reeking of Corona. "And I can tell you feel the same." A knowing smirk spread over his lips.

Alessandra took a deep breath and let out a husky laugh. "Yeah, right." Even though Jeremy was one of the better-looking men on campus, arrogant and sexy as hell, she would not let him take advantage of her. Not with the risks. Not even if her dreams *were* filled with visions of lapping every inch of his six-foot sculpted frame.

"I have class," she answered and took a step toward campus.

His hand clamped down on her arm, stopping her. "At least come to the party tonight. It's homecoming."

Alessandra sighed and chewed on her lip, considering his invitation. All her sorority sisters were going, along with everyone who was anyone on campus. She didn't think the grin on his face could get any bigger, but when she agreed, it widened. She looked at the hand clasped around her upper arm and he let go, taking a quick step back as she raised her gaze to his.

"It starts at eight." The wind kicked up, wrapping a cool breeze that promised a bitter winter, and he dug his hands into his pockets. "See you then." He turned and disappeared into the frat house.

ALESSANDRA FIDGETED IN HER seat through the entire class. Hunter texted at least a dozen times about a camping trip tonight, and she ignored each silent buzz of her phone.

Why did he always show up at the wrong time with the rest of his ragged pack? Her sweet sixteen, her first date, her prom—all screwed up for the sake of a "family" trip. Family? Ha! Not so much. More like unwanted chaperones. God, couldn't they let her have a normal life?

Her phone buzzed again, and she tore her gaze from the professor to the demanding words blinking on her phone. With a couple of quick keystrokes, she sent her defiant answer. She wasn't going this time. She'd meet up with them tomorrow. They could go one night without her leading the party.

She turned the phone off and focused back on the front of the classroom.

EVEN THE SIDEWALK VIBRATED from the hip-hop beat as she approached the front door of Alpha Beta Pi. She traded a glance with her sorority sisters, and they squeezed through the crowded house into the rear courtyard. Bodies crammed into the open space, moving like a sea of Mexican jumping beans.

She scanned the crowd and couldn't see Jeremy. A quick sniff brought several mingled scents, mostly booze and sweat, but another sweet scent laced the air: an undercurrent of marijuana—all the normal byproducts of a college frat party. Moments later, that musky aroma reached her, and she turned to see Jeremy approaching.

"Hey, Ally, want a beer?" He offered her one of the two opened Coronas in his hands.

"No thanks. I really shouldn't drink."

His eyebrows creased, and he bit his lip. "Why not? Are you an alcoholic or something?"

"Something like that."

The crease smoothed out, replaced by arches that rivaled McDonald's, and she chuckled at the incredulous look gracing his handsome, chiseled face.

"I'm actually allergic to alcohol."

The arches remained. "Really?" he grunted and handed the bottle to a wayward fraternity brother. "What, do you swell up like a balloon?"

This time, she laughed. "No, no spontaneous swelling." She didn't care to elaborate further.

"Want some punch instead?"

"Sure," she answered, licking her lips.

His gaze traveled between her mouth and her eyes, and he nodded, disappearing into the crowd. A few minutes later, he slipped next to her, handing her the plastic cup full of red fruit punch. A lovely orange ring decorated the edge, along with a glistening cherry.

She slid the cherry between her lips, severing it from the vine in such a way that he sucked in his breath, his chest rising and falling with the desire pumping through his blood, emitting a scent she adored, the tang of feral wanting.

Lifting the glass to her lips, she sipped the drink. Her thirst flared, and she downed the delectable liquid. "This is fantastic. What's in it?"

"Fruit punch, pineapple juice, Sprite, along with the fruit, of course," he answered. "Do you want me to get you some more?"

"Sure."

Before she knew it, he was back with a drink in each fist, both for her.

"This way, I don't have to run off again for at least another five minutes." He flashed his dazzling white teeth in her direction.

Halfway through the third glass, the room tilted, and she blinked, staring at the wavering liquid in her glass before bringing her gaze back to Jeremy's expectant grin.

"Why don't you finish that, and I'll take you outside? It's getting warm in here," he said, pointing to the glass, and she downed the rest and setting the glass on the nearest table.

Instead of heading out front as she expected, he pulled her up the stairs, corralling her out onto the balcony, and cornered her against the siding, pressing his body to hers, his lips finding the curve of her neck and his hands wandering over her silky shirt.

"Jeremy," she whispered, blinking away the slow spin that gripped her.

"What?" He brought his mouth away from her skin and raised a questioning eyebrow. His green eyes shimmered in the moonlight.

"What was in that drink?" Her tongue felt fuzzy in her mouth and she swallowed, scraping it along the dry roof of her mouth. She squelched the craving for another drink, especially considering her dulled senses. She struggled to perceive his musky scent or his beer-laced breath, even though he was inches away, and a constant buzz filled her ears, distorting all sound.

His grin widened, and his eyes twinkled. "It's a grain punch."

A measure of fear spun up her spine, chilling her warm skin. Her father's words echoed in her ear.

"Drinking will eliminate your ability to recognize trouble and stunt any opportunity you might have of escaping danger." His staunch parental glare punctuated the statement, and she never once questioned the hereditary reaction to alcohol.

After all, he had been right about everything else.

"Don't look so upset, angel. Enjoy the buzz." His lips found hers, drowning all her protests, drowning all logic, drowning all thoughts of her father's warning.

His kisses, along with the stroke of his hands and his whispered promises of forever, were as intoxicating as the drink, and she allowed him to lead her into his bedroom. The door latched behind them and he navigated her toward the bed. Helping her undress, his hands never stopped their exploration, fanning the flames in the pit of her stomach, and she matched his fervor, nipping at his neck and chest and stomach. He stopped her when she reached for his belt.

"I understand what you truly are." His sinuous tone filled her ear just before his tongue swiped it, sending chills through her lithe form. Before she could blink, he had her wrists bound behind her back and a blindfold covering her eyes.

"I know what you are." This time his voice held contempt and the back of his hand slammed into her cheekbone, sending her to the floor with flares of pain resonating through her jaw.

With her senses dulled with shock and alcohol, he yanked her to her feet and covered her with a rough blanket that reminded her of the old potato sacks they used to use for the sack races at camp rough and scratchy, to the point it itched. She struggled in the bonds.

She found her voice as the noise dissipated and she stumbled on the curb. "Jeremy, what the hell are you doing?"

The slide of a door dispelled her question, and he threw her into a cramped space. The clang of the door closing behind her confirmed her suspicions. She was inside the infamous Alpha Beta Pi van.

According to campus rumor, the fraternity brothers took turns filming their sexual encounters in this van. But she didn't think that's what he had in mind. No, she thought his motivations were a little darker than a sexual romp.

The van lurched forward, and hands tore the rough blanket from over her head. Lights bled from under the blindfold. "Jeremy?" She hated the twinge of fear in her voice.

The blindfold ripped from her face and she squinted under the intense lights. Blinking until her eyes adjusted, she made out his form just out of camera shot and he wasn't the one driving the van.

"What do we do with her?" someone behind Jeremy asked. She thought she recognized the voice, but before her brain could form a coherent thought, a needle jabbed into her leg.

Jeremy came out of the shadows and depressed the plunger, sending burning liquid up her thigh. Pain spread from the injection site, traveling through her system at mach speed. Her heart, already taxed by fear, pumped the poison through her bloodstream, creating a blazing agony in every cell of her being, and she screamed. The wail echoed through the small metal chamber and her muscles clenched into tight balls of anguish.

"Belladonna," he said, holding up the empty syringe. "That ought to keep her under control until the cougars find her," he said to the shadows over his shoulder.

Belladonna? Did he say Belladonna? Terror washed through her faster than the pain and her chest hitched breath after painful breath. Belladonna was one of the deadliest substances to her kind. This agony crippling her would only increase and if he spared her a fatal dose, at the very least, she wouldn't be able to function for the next few hours, never mind defend herself against this maniac.

"Why?" she hissed, straightening into a sitting position.

Sliding into the light, he crawled toward her like a predator. "Because I can't stand freaks of nature like you," he said, punctuating his statement with another backhand that sent her sprawling onto her side.

"Bastard."

His laugh filled the van, and he straddled her, the sound of multiple zippers barely audible above her ragged breath.

CLOSE TO TWO HOURS of rough sexual contact passed before the van pulled to a stop, gravel crunching under the wheels. Covered with their sweat, saliva, and semen, she nearly collapsed when they hauled her out of the van. Before she had a chance to recover and study her surroundings, the blindfold covered her eyes.

The late October wind lifted strands of her long black hair, whipping it around and smacking her face with each gust. Her once creamy skin turned into a relief map of gooseflesh among the bruises. Her feet protested with every sharp stone that pierced her sole. Each scratch of a branch tore at her skin, milking the pain and snapping her into instant sobriety.

Jeremy had a grip as strong as a vise on her upper arm, his fingers digging cruelly into her flesh. He dragged her along, impatiently correcting each of her stumbles with a yank.

Hot tears stung her eyes and coated the back of her throat; she stifled the sob, locking it in her chest. Her muscles still hadn't recovered from the Belladonna or the brutal rape she endured, but she refused to collapse. Not here, not in the mountains. Not with the wild cats roaming these woods, just looking for the chance to rip someone like her to pieces.

The sudden lack of sticks digging against her along with the soft moss-like grass underfoot signaled a break in the forest. Dull light bled under her blindfold, the full harvest moon illuminating the clearing. They walked another hundred paces from the wood line before they stopped.

Her bound wrists yanked toward the ground, almost knocking her to her knees, and then the slack returned and her hands again rested at the small of her back.

Shivering in the night wind, she stuttered, "W-w-what are y-you d-d-oing?" Her teeth chattered through every word.

"Setting the bait," Jeremy whispered close to her ear. His breath caressed her cheek and then a cool substance spread from the crown of her head, dripping through her hair, covering her bare skin, tickling as it traced paths down her legs. The air filled with a sweet tang, reminding her of a fine cut of venison cooking on the grill and she licked her lips despite the bone chilling cold settling into her already exhausted limbs.

It took a second to recognize the substance, and between the flavor on her lips and the overwhelming scents accosting her, primal fear jump-started her adrenaline. "What are you doing?" The shiver was less pronounced as panic overtook her senses.

Another prick pierced her shoulder, and the pain flared again. "If the mountain lions don't kill you first, the wolves will. They always attack my poisoned offerings and when they do, the Belladonna in your system will kill them just as surely as it'll kill you."

The shuffle of feet followed his harsh statement, their pattern speeding up and drawing farther away.

"You son of a bitch!" she called after them, taking a step toward the diminishing noise. Her bound arms stopped her, anchored to something in the clearing. She struggled to break the binds. She battled against the burning poison traveling through her bloodstream and she struggled against the need to curl up into a tight ball of agony.

Barely able to remain standing, she dropped to her knees. "I will kill you!" Alessandra cried once more and then listened until the distinct footfalls on the forest floor vanished, along with their laughter. A car ignition sparked, followed by the fading sound of the engine. A sob welled up from her bowels, the long forlorn moan echoing in the small clearing, cascading over the trees into the heart of the forest, a calling to the carnivores searching for sustenance.

Adrenaline faded, and her teeth chattered, the cold soaking through her skin again and leaving her numb. Rolling her shoulder, she attempted to dislodge the blindfold, failing. After a few tries, an exasperated growl escaped between the constant click of her teeth.

An owl let out a screeching hoot and her heart lurched in her chest, her whole body following suit. The cry of a wildcat in the distance set her heart into a frantic beat, one that left her dizzy and warm despite the cold.

Fear-laced rage wound around her, and she forced herself to her feet. She didn't want to die out here in the woods. Not at the claws of a wild beast, not on the eve of the harvest moon. A guttural roar of frustration leaped from her lips and she struggled to break the binds holding her in place, but the rope wouldn't budge. "Son of a bitch!" she repeated over and over and over at the top of her lungs until she had no voice left.

That's when the leaves shuffled under padded feet.

Alessandra crouched low to the ground, bringing her face to her knees, praying and shimmying the blindfold far enough to uncover her eyes. Gleaming bones, whole rib cages and skulls, along with disembodied arms and legs, littered the ground around her and her breath hitched in her chest.

Anchored to a metal bar planted in concrete in the center of the perfectly round clearing, she studied the discolored rope binding her in place. Glimmering black liquid dripped from the twine.

The shakes that gripped her this time around were not from the cold.

The ground surrounding her feet was soaked with blood. It pooled in small divots, shimmering black in the moonlight. It dripped from her torso down her legs, and it filled the night with a succulent scent of fallen prey. Marked with deer blood, she was fair game to the scavengers in the woods.

Thoughts of bears and any manner of wild cats, especially cougars, made her skin break out with droplets of perspiration, announcing her fear to any beast surrounding the clearing.

She raised her eyes to the wood line. Golden eyes peered out from the dark, dozens of them, and a low grumble surfaced in unison. Her eyes darted to the bones on the ground and back to the eyes.

The first wolf stepped into the clearing, baring his teeth and keeping his dark hungry eyes locked with Alessandra's. The mammoth wolf stood close to six feet, his fur a mass of gray, black, and white markings swirled together to form a pelt worthy of a hunter's gun.

Alessandra stopped shaking and struggling with the binds around her wrist. "Come on." The words came out in a low rumble from her chest and the wolf paused, its slow stalk forward, halting, his teeth no longer bared.

The pack stepped into the circle, lining the woods.

Alessandra broke the stare with the alpha wolf, glancing around the clearing and counting. She brought her focus back to the first animal, tilting her head slightly. There were fifteen wolves, including the magnificent gray wolf in front of her. They sniffed the air, bringing their tails between their legs, and lowered their heads in unison. A low growl broke the silence.

The mighty beast resumed his approach, slowly crossing the distance alone. The rest of the pack hung back, watching their leader.

He sniffed the blood surrounding her feet and lapped at it without breaking eye contact, the rumble still building in his throat.

Alessandra dropped to her knees in front of the wolf. "Hunter, get me the hell out of these binds," she whispered.

The harvest moon reflected red in the wolf's eyes as they moved from her face to the soft tissue of her neck.

"Belladonna," Alessandra warned, causing the wolf to return his gaze to hers.

His eyes widened in understanding and sadness filled the deep blue eyes.

"You can't bite me. None of you can. If you do, you'll die, too."

Teeth grazed her wrists, and she cut her gaze back at the pristine white pelt of another wolf. Its powerful jaws clamped on the rope, and she offered a half-baked tilt of her lips to the silver eyes before she focused back on Hunter.

The pack closed the distance but was too skittish to partake in the spilled blood surrounding Alessandra, the blood the gray wolf lapped, his tongue soaking up the thick substance with each stroke before it disappeared between his giant teeth.

"It's okay," she whispered, glancing at the circle.

Tentatively, they lowered their snouts to the blood and began to drink.

The ties holding her wrists loosened, and she shifted so the white wolf could break the binding the rest of the way. A few minutes later, she rubbed her wrists, scanning the surrounding pack.

"There is a way." She stood. She traded a glance with Hunter, and his eyes narrowed in dissent. Even so, when she stood, they parted, letting her through. Without looking back, she walked into the thick woods, her head tilted low, her teeth grinding together and her eyes glimmering with the red moon.

She had a score to settle and before she stepped out of the woods onto the edge of the road, she tilted her head back, letting out a haunting howl. The pack followed suit.

She lifted her nose to the air and caught the scent, heading in the same direction they had a few hours earlier after leaving her in the clearing. Jeremy mentioned a camping trip tonight. That was before he drugged her, before he bound her and left her for dead.

She walked, ignoring the burning ache in her muscles and the sharp pain in her feet, heading downwind and reaching their campsite at almost four in the morning. She didn't have much more time before the Belladonna seized her heart, leaving her in a death spasm. His musky scent mingled with the smoke of burning pine and hickory was a welcomed relief.

They were still up, laughing and toasting their success at bringing another shape-shifter into the woods, wondering how long she lasted before the animals attacked and if anyone heard her dying screams.

She stopped, still hidden by the thickets, her anger coiling inside, warming her near frozen skin. Reaching her hand out, she found Hunter's soft fur at her fingertips. Stroking his massive head, his tongue flicked her calf, cleaning a small patch of dried blood from her silky skin.

"I am aware we made a promise, but it's the one and only method that will counter Belladonna," she whispered under the crackling of the fire. She slashed her gaze to his deep blue eyes. "It's the only thing that'll save me, and that bastard deserves it."

She whistled at a frequency too low for the human ear, sending out her command. The pack silently padded through the woods surrounding the clearing.

She stepped into the opening, accompanied by the mammoth gray wolf.

The laughter died as three pairs of wide eyes stared in her direction.

Jeremy shot to his feet, eyes darting between a blood-soaked Alessandra and her companion. He put his hands out in front of him. "You, you, you should be dead," he said, taking a step back. A wet spot spread across the front of his jeans, filling the air with an acrid stench mingled with fear.

The full moon hung low in the sky as the collective growl of the pack filled the clearing and they stepped into view, blocking any chance of escape.

The alcohol that prohibited her from transforming had finally worked its way through her system, and Alessandra broke out in a feral grin. Cocking her head, her teeth transitioned from blunt incisors to razor-sharp fangs.

"You *do* know human blood counteracts Belladonna, right?" Her teeth gleamed in the moonlight; the long canines glistened, saliva dripping at the prospect of her next meal.

Chapter 1

ALESSANDRA TATE STOOD ON the balcony of the old cabin, staring out into the woods with a cup of hot chocolate in her hands. Her thoughts kept drifting to the night she was attacked. As much as she wished she could shut the memories down, they kept crawling to the surface. She shivered. Hands came to rest on her shoulders, and she jumped, nearly spilling the scalding liquid down the front of her.

"How are you doing?" Hunter's deep baritone whispered.

His concern grated on her nerves. "Fine," she said, even though she was anything but. She had crossed the line and was now a fugitive. Killing a human for any reason was taboo.

The tribal community didn't care that Jeremy and his fraternity brothers had beaten and raped her. They didn't care. The bastard had injected her with belladonna and left her for dead.

All they cared about was that she had spilled human blood.

"Bull," he said.

She turned. Hunter's sharp blue eyes held her gaze. He was as handsome a man as he was a wolf, but she had always seen him as her right hand, her beta in charge of the pack when she wasn't around. She had alpha blood running through her veins. Hunter Blaez didn't.

Besides, he was six years older, and had always viewed her like a little sister who needed to be protected. The night they attacked her, he crossed the line with her, tearing into those frat boys with as much feral fury as she had, while the rest of the pack looked on in horror.

The only reason she was alive today was because of the human hearts she'd ingested.

That was the only thing that reversed the deadly effects of the belladonna.

"Why did you do it?" she asked, searching his eyes.

His lips twitched, and his eyes honed to the woods, scanning the trees as if the answers she was looking for were carved into the bark. When his gaze returned, he sighed and gave her a single shoulder shrug.

Hunter wasn't much for small talk, and Alessandra had been thankful for that during the days following the massacre, but that was three months ago. Now, his quiet demeanor just made her want to scream and shake him. She needed more than silence and sullen glances.

It was one reason she had fled her home to go to college.

She needed active participation in conversations, not blind followers.

She needed someone who would debate issues with her.

She needed someone who challenged her.

"Hunter, talk to me," she said, using the alpha tone he had to obey.

He snarled and turned away. "I hate it when you do that."

"Why did you spill their blood when you didn't have to?"

"Because what they did to you pissed me off." He glanced over his shoulder at her, with eyes full of hellfire. "Shits like that don't deserve to live." He ran his hand through his dark hair. Hunter's mouth opened as if he wanted to say more, but then his lips clamped together.

Alessandra set the hot chocolate on the table and crossed her arms. "And?"

He stalked to where she stood, towering over her. "If you haven't figured it out by now, you're as blind as you are naïve." He spun and disappeared into the house, leaving her staring after him.

She charged in after him. "What the hell does that mean?"

He stopped halfway up the stairwell. "Ally..."

"No, Hunter. I need to know. I need to understand why the hell you would damn yourself to a life on the run?"

"I didn't want you going through this alone. Besides, your innocence wasn't theirs to take."

She didn't disagree, but there was something deeper in his gaze, more personal. He trudged up the stairs without saying more.

"Hunter?"

He stopped but didn't turn.

Alessandra wanted to push him for more, but the tight set of his shoulders kept her quiet. "I don't think I've ever said thank you," she finally said.

His slow up and down tilt of his chin warmed the chill between them, and then he disappeared into his room.

She blinked as the conversation settled into her and his words finally sank in. She crossed to his door on the far side of the house. Hunter had his back to her and was in the middle of peeling his sweater off. His muscles rippled as he tossed the garment into his hamper.

"What do you mean by 'if I haven't figured out by now'?"

He spun in her direction, and she stared at his bare chest and carved six-pack. Alessandra tried to recall the last time she'd seen him bare-chested. She thought it might have been when she was in middle school and he was a senior in high school. His physique distracted her, and she completely forgot the question she just asked.

"You really don't understand, do you?"

Her gaze snapped from his chest to his eyes. "Huh?"

He raised an eyebrow.

Alessandra shook her head to clear her mind. "I don't understand what?"

Hunter crossed to the door and grabbed the doorframe with his hands, blocking her from entering farther. "You don't want to get into this with me right now."

His tone ruffled the alpha in her, and she straightened with a glare. "Yes. I do."

"Alessandra," he said, his tone held a warning as clear as the use of her full name. He dropped his arms and stepped back, putting distance between them.

She encroached on his space. "Hunter, what is with you?"

His jaw clicked closed and the blaze in his eyes turned feral. "You can't be this close to me right now."

"Why not?"

"Because," he growled, and his hands curled into fists.

Alessandra looked up into his electric blue eyes and something inside her fluttered. His musky scent mixed with the aggravation radiating from him. "Because why?" Her question came out in a soft whisper.

"Because I can't get that shit out of my head. I wasn't there to stop them, and it burns more than you can fathom. Every night I hear you screaming in your sleep and that just magnifies my failure." He turned away from her and his hands slowly uncurled.

The tension in his back remained, and she reached out, placing her palm on his shoulder.

"I was the one who blew you off that night. It's not your fault."

Hunter sighed. "I should have been close enough to do something," he whispered. "I should have known."

Alessandra stepped to his side, taking in his profile. He side-eyed her, but he didn't turn to meet her gaze. "Hunter, there was no way you could have known. I didn't even sense it until it was too late."

His lashes brushed his cheeks. "You were too absorbed in trying to be normal to sense the danger."

His tone was harsh enough to draw her hand away from his skin. Hunter glared sideways. "You are always too caught up in Alessandra to see anything beyond your narrow view."

"What the hell..."

He turned, grabbed her by the arms, and slammed her against the wall, pressing his form to her with a low growl. "I've always been your equal in speed and strength out there." He jutted his chin towards the window. "And I did a damned good job leading the pack while you were away, but you never even acknowledged it. Just like you've never acknowledged this."

Alessandra stared wide-eyed into his angry features, but that wasn't what clouded her mind. It was his hard body pressed against hers, all of it, including parts she had never associated with her beta. She gasped as his hips pressed into her, making his point clear.

"That is what you do to me. Now, do you understand why I damned myself alongside you?"

Alessandra couldn't speak, she just searched his eyes. Flashes of pain and want echoed in his irises like a warning signal, and her breath hitched.

"They took what I have wanted for years. They hurt you in ways I don't have a clue how to heal. They made it so that when I brush against you, you flinch. That is harder than your naïve ignorance ever was."

"I just never..." Alessandra started.

Hunter lowered her and stepped away. "You never saw me. I get it." He put his hands up, increasing his distance.

She blinked and took him in as if staring at a stranger. "That's not it. I guess I always assumed your interest lay elsewhere, so the thought of you and me being more than just an alpha and her second in command never entered my mind."

His eyes narrowed. "But you see me now, right?" He held his arms wide.

Heat filled Alessandra's cheeks. "It's kind of hard not to."

His lips thinned as he pressed them together like he was trying to keep a comment to himself. He rolled his eyes and reached for the t-shirt on the edge of the bed.

When he covered his chiseled chest, a measure of disappointment filled her. That reaction sent a jolt of electricity from her fingertips right into the center of her soul. She had never viewed him as mate material before, and now that he had finally laid his true intentions out before her, it sparked a fiery current. One that she was deathly afraid of.

Alessandra took a step backwards, putting a buffer of space between them, and Hunter sighed.

"Really?"

Her eyes darted around the room as the discomfort built inside her like a wildfire, turning her confidence into fear. The panic attack squeezed her lungs and all her mind focused on was the abuse she'd endured in the van. The thought of another man touching her made her stomach roll, and she bolted into the hallway and nearly dove at the toilet in her bathroom, reaching it just in time for the contents of her stomach to paint the bowl.

"This is why I shredded their throats," Hunter said from behind her.

His hands gently pulled her hair away from her face and he kneeled beside her, rubbing her back as the memories overwhelmed her once more.

Chapter 2

HUNTER SAT IN THE dark, staring out into the deep woods. He had cleaned Alessandra up and tucked her into bed before retiring to the living room and the fifth of vodka he had stashed away. Alcohol wasn't a werewolf's friend, as Alessandra had found out. It shut down their senses and made it impossible to shift.

But it was also something that numbed the pain.

Alessandra's reaction tonight was not what he thought it would be. He thought by now she would have warmed up to him, or at least have seen the possibilities, especially with the spark that had filled her eyes at the sight of him shirtless.

Instead, the thought of being with him made her vomit.

He scoffed, and drained the glass, letting the bite of the vodka settle his nerves.

"What the hell did you expect?" he asked his reflection. No answer came, so he filled the glass and repeated, grimacing at the slow burn sliding down his esophagus.

He downed another drink and picked up the bottle, pouring the last few drops into his glass. His hands tingled, as did his cheeks, and he let out an enormous sigh.

"Hunter?"

He stiffened on the couch but didn't turn. The fact he hadn't heard her pad down the stairs or caught her scent in the air gave testament to the risks of alcohol for their kind.

She stepped into view, her gaze glued to the now empty bottle. Instead of drowning in the last half glass himself, he offered it to her.

She stared at it before shaking her head.

"Suit yourself." He hammered the last of the vodka back and slammed the glass on the table.

"What are you doing?"

"Getting shitfaced." He licked his numb lips. "Duh." Her incredulous look crawled under his inebriated skin. "Don't look so disappointed."

"I just..." She waved at him.

"You just what? You just thought I'd stick my tail between my legs and follow you around like I have for the last ten years?" Sarcasm rang in his voice. "Just be a good boy and not make any waves?" Anger flared at the rise in her eyebrows. "Fuck you."

She huffed, and instead of glaring at her, he returned his gaze to the world outside.

"I've wasted ten years, hoping you'd come around, and when I finally tell you what's in my head, the thought of being with me makes you throw up," he growled and stood. The ground seemed to shift, and he reached for the couch to steady himself. "I damned myself for you. What a fucking idiot."

He stumbled to the sliders and opened the door to an arctic blast of air. He shivered and turned in her direction.

"So, just keep your opinion to yourself right now, because I don't need a lecture or some bullshit excuse. I needed a drink, so I had one."

"Do you get what they did to me?" she asked, her voice holding controlled anger.

"I don't care." Hunter went to step outside.

"You understand what a gang bang is, right?"

He paused, fighting his own memories of their stench saturating every cell, making her reek. The demons were back, and his stomach lurched. He reached the railing and leaned over, using the cold wood to catch his breath and calm the violent spasm in his belly.

"They made me swallow their dicks until I choked. They fucked me until I bled from both my vagina and my ass, but that didn't stop them. They continued to rotate until they were too tired to get it up anymore."

Hunter spun towards her. "I know," he bellowed, as his fists clenched.

"Then how the hell can you possibly think I would willingly let another man touch me ever again?" she yelled back, her voice echoing off the thick pines.

Hunter blinked, and his hands uncurled as the depths of her pain squeezed his heart to the breaking point. He didn't know how to answer her, or how to erase the horrors. But he had to try.

With a speed that belied his drunkenness, he closed the distance and pulled her into his arms, crushing her lips under his. She gasped and went rigid in his arms. He took advantage of the situation, dipping his tongue into her open mouth, tasting a hint of the mint toothpaste she had used.

The snarl that came from her, along with a shove that sent him across the porch, stopped his heart cold. She shifted in a blink and darted towards him with her teeth bared. Instead of cowering like he should have, he jumped to his feet and charged at her, still in human form.

Anger pulsed in his temples and he ducked under her snap and turned, throwing himself on her back, wrapping his arm around her neck in the process and dragged her to the ground with him. He held her spine to his chest and clamped his hand around her snout.

"Don't you dare bite me," he growled in her ear. "You may have been the alpha queen of the pack, but you aren't running a pack anymore."

She tried to dislodge her snout by shaking her head.

"It's just you and me, but I'll gladly leave you the hell alone if you keep this shit up."

She stopped moving, even relaxed against him. He loosened his grip. She twisted and stood over him with her teeth bared, the feral growl shocking him as much as her limberness had.

Hunter stared into her fiery eyes. "Go ahead." He leaned his head back, exposing his throat.

Her growl subsided, and she licked her chops before letting out a huff. She settled on top of him, nuzzling her nose under his chin. He took a deep breath and sighed, wrapping his arms around her.

He stroked her silky fur while staring at the stars above them. After a few minutes, he lifted her muzzle, making her meet his gaze. "I'm not subservient to you. If you want me to stay, we are equals," he said. "If you don't want me, then you have to cut me loose."

Her soft whine shot his nerves, leaving them raw and exposed.

"I can't stay if there is no future here." He rolled her off and headed inside. The alcohol hadn't numbed the pain piercing his heart.

"Hunter?"

He turned, taking in her tear-stained face.

She stumbled, and then the sound of the gunshot echoed. Red spread across her shoulder and his breath locked in his throat. He moved, tackling her before a second shot shattered the glass door.

She panted in his ear as he rolled her out of the sightline of the woods. His chest constricted and he could hardly pull air into his lungs. His gaze shot to the opposite side of the cottage where the car keys sat on the counter, and the door to the garage where their jeep had sat for the last couple of months. He had no idea if it would even start, but if they didn't hightail it out of here, they would be dead.

"Looks like our brief reprieve is up," he said, and met her gaze. "Time to run." He pulled her to her feet, and she winced. With her hand clasped in his, he darted across the opening, using the furniture as a barrier. He didn't slow down as he passed the counter, swiping the keys and catapulting both of them through the garage door.

Darkness flooded his vision, and he cursed the alcohol he'd just drunk. Without it, he was truly human, truly without the extra wolf's senses that kept him alive and out of danger. The buzz evaporated the moment Alessandra had launched at him, and now his heart pumped with a frantic need to purge the drug from his system, but he ignored the burn of it and swung the door open.

Alessandra climbed in and he bolted to the driver's side, fumbling with the keys. He slid them in the ignition and closed his eyes, saying a little prayer before he turned the key. The jeep jumped to life and Hunter didn't wait for the garage doors to open. Instead, he pressed down hard on the accelerator, hitting the center of the barn-style doors, knocking them wide and scraping the sides of the jeep.

He flipped on his bright lights, hoping to blind anyone wearing night vision goggles. He tore down the road, almost standing on the gas pedal. His knowledge of the roads and all the possible escape routes proved essential, and they didn't encounter anyone, which meant they had attacked from the woods, not the road.

"You okay?" he asked when they were a fair distance away and his heart rate had finally come back to normal.

Her wheezing pulled his attention from the road. He nearly ran off the blacktop at the sight of her struggling to breathe. Hunter pulled off at the next turnaround and slammed the brakes, shifting the vehicle into park before he gave her his full attention.

"Silver." Alessandra barely whispered, and Hunter reached into the back seat, pulling out the first aid kit he had stowed away.

His hands shook as he ripped through the package, looking for the scalpel. That bullet would kill her as surely as the belladonna would have if he didn't get it the hell out of her. Metal glinted, and he grabbed the scalpel, his heart slamming back home now that he had a means to dig it out.

The dread in her eyes revealed that she was already aware this was going to be painful, so instead of wasting words, he tore her shirt off and examined the wound. The blood on the front of her shirt was not an exit wound. It was from splintered fragments of her shoulder and collarbone.

"Shit," he muttered and met her gaze. "Stay in this form, no matter how much this hurts. Okay?" He waited for her nod and then went to work. She cried out, but to her credit, she did not squirm under the pressure.

Sweat speckled her forehead and the tightness of her jaw was enough to rip another patch of his heart, but he finally pulled the silver out with his fingers, ignoring the fiery burn against his skin. He looked at the cause of her agony and let out a snarl as he pitched it out the window.

"Drive," she whispered.

"I need to patch you up first."

"No. Drive. Trust me; they are close enough for me to catch a scent on the wind." Her weak voice tore his resolve, and he slid back into the seat, doing exactly as she asked until they were another fifteen minutes down the road. He turned off on a barely visible side road, parking under an overgrown pine thicket. The dull green of the jeep blended in, and he prayed they were hidden enough for him to stitch her up.

He turned on the overhead light, hating the fact he needed it. Alessandra's face was bathed in sweat and her eyes had that dull quality of shock.

"I have nothing to give you," he said, and pulled a needle and thread from the medical kit. With a deep breath, he leaned in and began the painstaking work of closing her wounds.

"I'm glad you're a doctor," she whispered as he pulled the last stitch.

He delivered her a small chuckle and met her gaze. "I never actually finished my residency."

Her eyebrows arched and he offered her a shrug.

"I only had a couple of weeks left and my final medical exam had already been scheduled..." He placed a bandage over the stitches before packing up the medical kit and stowing it away in the back seat. "But then everything went to hell... And here we are."

Hunter flipped the overhead light off and slid back into the driver's seat.

"I'm sorry. I didn't know," Alessandra whispered.

He huffed and put the car in drive. He had no idea where to go next. This was the only safe house he had bought after his father went missing, and while he had an exit strategy in place, he had hoped they wouldn't need it, because he was all out of ideas.

"Just get some rest," he said, trying to keep the annoyance churning in his stomach alongside the vodka from creeping into his voice, but he failed.

"What is your issue?" she asked.

"I can't fucking see. I can't catch a scent, either. Not with the damned alcohol in my system, and I have no idea where the hell to go."

"What about—"

"—There's nowhere left for us to go." He sent her a glare that matched his tone. With the edge of the vodka fading, anger replaced it with a relentless burn.

"No need to get bitchy. After all, I was the one who got shot," she snapped.

He swerved off the main road, barely staying on the blacktop of a nearly hidden road. The jeep jumped with every pothole and frost heave, jostling them both in the seats. The hiss from between her teeth pulled his glance her way, and he eased up on the gas pedal.

"Sorry," he muttered.

"It's okay," she said, her voice soft and full of the pain he was sure was pummeling her shoulder.

"Motel or side of the road?" he asked.

She remained silent for longer than he expected. When he looked her way, she sighed.

She sucked her lower lip between her teeth and met his gaze. "What is safer?"

"Damned if I know."

Alessandra scanned the wooded landscape. "Think we could break into one of these cabins?"

"I don't want to leave fresh tracks in the snow." He focused on the road. "But if I come across something that already has tracks, maybe that's an option."

"Is that really wise?"

He huffed a laugh. "None of the options are wise, but we might be able to get away with holding up in a cabin with people. It could mask our scents and it's something they wouldn't look for. Besides, we can say we are almost out of gas and saw the tracks. Instead of freezing out in the car…"

She kept chewing on her lip. "How do you explain this?" Ally nodded at her shoulder.

"You need to change and we need to bury the clothes in the snow."

"You've got blood on you, too."

"Then we both change." He pulled the jeep to the side and got out, making his way to the back where the emergency bag sat. It held clothes for at least a couple of days. He shuffled through the clothing, pulling out jeans and a sweater for Alessandra and a clean sweater for himself. He stripped his blood-splattered shirt and tossed it on the ground behind the jeep before going to the passenger door. "Do you need some help?" he asked, as he handed her the spare clothes.

Alessandra shook her head and shimmied on her pants under the nightshirt she wore. Hunter turned away, but her sharp intake of breath pulled him back around. She had the shirt partially off and was struggling to get her injured arm and head out of the cloth. He reached in and gently pulled it over her head, exposing her bare chest.

Hunter focused on getting the fabric off her shoulder, but the awareness that her perky breasts were inches away from his hands sent a tremor of heat through him. He dropped the bloody shirt on the ground outside and picked up the sweater from her lap, helping her to thread her injured arm into the sleeve before slipping the shirt over her head.

At that moment, he stole a glance at her sweet chest. Desire boiled in his blood and he forced himself to step back. If he stayed that close, he would do something he would regret. Instead, he picked up her nightshirt and closed the passenger door.

With every step away from the door, the burn inside him cooled. Hunter collected his shirt and jogged the way they'd come until he found what he was looking for. A snow bank big enough to hide their scent.

He squatted and started digging at the frozen snow until he had a sufficient tunnel for the two shirts. With numb fingers, he shoved the clothing as deep as it would go before filling in the hole. By the time he got back to the jeep, his hands were numb enough to sting from the warm air of the car.

Squeezing and opening his fists, he got the blood pumping until his hands tingled. Finally, he glanced at Alessandra. "Feeling better?"

She shook her head. "That really hurt."

"Just hang in there. I'll find us a safe place to get some rest. Okay?" Alessandra needed sleep to heal and being in this car would not give her the opportunity to rest. All she needed was eight hours of deep sleep and that gunshot wound would be gone. By that time, he would be back to himself as well, and no longer vulnerable like he was without his wolf's senses.

Chapter 3

IT TOOK HUNTER ANOTHER hour and a half to find a place that was occupied and had a driveway only big enough for one set of tire tracks. He carefully traced over the same tracks until he got to the garage, and instead of pulling up behind the garage, he pulled into a space next to it that would keep their vehicle hidden from the road.

"How many?"

Alessandra sniffed the air. "Four. One adult and three kids."

"Damn. A family is less likely to help."

She closed her eyes and concentrated, focusing on her good hand. Feeling the transformation start, she swung, catching his forearm, leaving four deep slices.

"Jesus," he gasped and grabbed his bleeding limb as she reined the beast back, pushing it down inside her. "What the hell did you do that for?"

"Take your shoes off," she demanded, and he did as she asked. "Now they'll help." She climbed out of the car before he could comment and waited for him to step by her side. He stared at her, holding onto his bleeding arm, and they continued to the front door. With a deep breath and a quick glance at Hunter, she knocked and waited.

She knocked again, this time getting herself set to pour out a fictional story about camping and a run in with a bear. It would also give her an excuse for why she was barefoot in the snow. A hasty retreat from a tent... and voilà.

Lights came on and she braced herself. "Just follow my lead," she said to Hunter before the door opened.

A man with a shotgun and sleep-tousled hair stood on the other side of the door.

"Oh, thank god!" Alessandra said, her voice full of panic along with a hint of relief. "My boyfriend got attacked by a bear while we were camping and I've been driving forever looking for someone to be home. I prayed that the tracks to this cottage were people coming in and not going out. Can you help us?" She kept shifting her feet, and he finally looked down.

His eyebrows rose and his gaze jumped to Hunter.

Hunter held his arm close to his chest and shrugged. "We kind of left everything in the tent, and then she proceeded to get very lost."

He lowered the shotgun a fraction, and the man glanced over his shoulder before looking back at the two of them.

"Maybe we should keep on trying to find a gas station?" Hunter said, looking at her and shifting his feet.

Alessandra looked from Hunter to the man inside. "Can you point us in the right direction?" she asked, knowing that the closest one had to be a fair distance away. Far enough for her not to pick up any gasoline scent on the light wind shuffling their clothing.

He lowered the gun a little more. "The nearest one is about thirty miles to the north. You just take a right out of the driveway and keep going."

Alessandra turned to Hunter. "I think we have enough gas to get there," she said. "Thank you," she said to the man, sending her warmest disarming smile in his direction before she turned to head back to the car.

"Wait a second," the man said, lowering the gun all the way. "What's your gas gauge on?"

Alessandra chewed her bottom lip and her gaze bounced between Hunter and the man in the doorway. "It's on E, but the light hasn't gone on yet."

The man ran his hand down his face and then sighed. "Look, I'm not comfortable with strangers in my house, but I can't, in good conscience, send you off when an empty gas tank in anything worth a damn on these roads won't make it thirty miles on empty." He stepped aside and waved for us to come in. "Why don't you come in and we can look at your friend's arm, and then we can figure out what to do about your car situation."

Alessandra gave him a grateful smile and entered the house, glad to be out of the cold. She turned when the door closed. Hunter stood on the entry tile, giving her a raised eyebrow. Her gaze dropped to her wet bare feet, leaving an imprint in the plush fibers, and she nearly jumped back onto the tile.

"Do you happen to have a towel and a first aid kit?" Hunter asked.

"You don't need to stand by the door, son. Why don't you come in and take a seat," the man said.

"I don't want to ruin your carpet," Hunter replied.

The homeowner gave him a once over. "Well, then, I best get to it." He stepped into the far hallway.

Alessandra looked at Hunter. His face had lost most of the bright color it had when he got back in the jeep after making them change. He leaned against the door, meeting her gaze with a trace of a smile.

She stepped towards him. "Are you okay?"

"I'll be fine," he said, but he certainly didn't look fine.

"Maybe you should sit."

"That's not a bad idea. The adrenaline is definitely fading." He slowly slid down to the floor and crossed his legs. "Way too much excitement for one night," he mumbled.

Alessandra let out a soft chuckle. He wasn't kidding. She was just as exhausted as he looked, and her shoulder pounded. Sleep was beginning to be a necessity, not just something nice, and she yawned.

"I'm tired, too," Hunter said, just as the man came out with a couple of towels and a first aid kit.

"The name's Stan," he said, handing a towel to Alessandra and then to Hunter.

"I'm Hunter, and my girlfriend's name is Ally," Hunter said, pointing in her direction.

The way he said girlfriend sent a warm flush through Alessandra and she tilted the edges of her lips ingo a semblance of a smile to mask the chill Hunter had created in her. It was almost as shocking a reaction as the way his lips had felt earlier.

"Let's look at that arm." Stan crouched down next to Hunter, inspecting the tears in his shirt. "You might need to take that off in order for us to get an idea of the severity of the wounds."

He attempted to shed the sweater and got his arm stuck in the fabric. Alessandra moved closer to help like he had done for her. Her hand grazed his skin as she peeled the sweater over his head and the connection lit a fire inside her. One that scared the shit out of her. His words from earlier echoed in her ears and she moved back so Stan could take a look at the damage she'd done to Hunter.

"I'm not sure I have what you need in this box," Stan said.

Alessandra eyed the cuts. She had gone deeper than she meant to.

"At least it wasn't my throat," Hunter said, trying to lighten the mood as he inspected the wounds. "I'll just need to clean the wounds and use some butterfly Band-Aids." He sucked on his lower lip and turned his eyes upwards, meeting Alessandra's gaze. "If you have a small tube of liquid band-aid, that would help as well."

"All I have is what's in this kit," Stan said, and flipped open the case.

Hunter took a deep breath and laid the towel across his lap. "Do you have hydrogen peroxide?"

Stan shook his head.

"Whiskey?" Hunter asked.

Stan nodded and disappeared into the kitchen.

"You're not drinking that, are you?" Alessandra asked.

Hunter' shoulders jerked in a sloppy shrug. "That might dull the pain when I flush the wounds with it."

The sting of irritation raked through her, but the flash in his eyes daring her to say more kept her silent. She had caused his pain. All of it, and nothing she could say would stop him from his current self-destructive path. At least nothing she was willing to admit to.

Stan came back with the bottle and handed it to Hunter. Alessandra pressed her lips together as he unscrewed the bottle. The man actually hesitated and closed his eyes for a second. When he opened his eyes, his blue irises shone, and he clenched his jaw, pouring the scotch across his arm. Air hissed between his teeth. Then he brought the bottle to his lips and took a hefty sip before handing it back.

"Thanks," he said, and then patted the broken skin with the towel, blotting both blood and alcohol from the wounds. Hunter looked at Alessandra. "I need you to put the butterfly band-aids across the cuts where I tell you."

Alessandra stepped closer, putting his shirt next to him on the floor. Both she and Stan fished through the kit, pulling out a dozen of the small elastic sutures. They carefully patched Hunter's arm at his direction, and when the worst of the wounds were closed, they wrapped his arm in gauze from his wrist to his elbow.

"That should do it," he said as Alessandra taped the end of the gauze with a small band-aid. "Thanks," he added.

Stan stood, gathered the remnants of their triage session. "I have a guest room downstairs, if you two want to catch some sleep. We can figure out what to do about gas in the morning."

Her gaze linked with Hunter's and she gave Stan a nod. If he had meant them harm, he probably would have done something by now. "That would be nice. I think, now that the adrenaline has faded, we both could use a little rest before we deal with anything else."

"Much appreciated." Hunter climbed to his feet.

Stan brought them into a partially finished basement that held a double bed. He waved towards the opposite corner. "There's a powder room over there where you can clean up. There're a couple of hand towels for you. The bed's already made. My son's friends are supposed to be swinging in tomorrow, so..."

"We hope to be out of your hair before your guests arrive," Hunter said. "Thank you for your hospitality. It is a rare quality these days."

Stan's cheeks bloomed at the compliment. He left them to their own devices, closing the door at the top of the stairs. The click of the lock caught her attention.

"He doesn't trust us," she said.

Hunter lay on his back on the bed. "He's just being cautious." He waved toward the bulkhead doors to their right. "We can still get out, but with the door upstairs locked, we can't get to his family. He's compassionate, but not blind to what could happen."

Alessandra stood staring at the small bed, and Hunter sprawled out on the mattress. Finally, he lifted his head and met her gaze.

"I'm not sleeping on the bare floor," he said, and she cocked an eyebrow at him. "We both need sleep to heal. I'm not tossing and turning on the floor, so you choose. You can share the bed with me, or you can have the floor."

"What if I order you?"

He slowly sat up. "If you order me? What the fuck? I saved your ass tonight. I deserve a soft mattress. Don't worry, princess, I'm not in the mood for anything other than sleep tonight."

"Hunter," she started.

"Once I get you somewhere safe, I'm not sticking around," he said, and rolled to his side, giving her a view of his back.

Alessandra stared at the remaining space on the bed and then the hard industrial carpet on the floor. Instead of immediately dealing with the situation, she stepped into the bathroom to relieve herself and wash up as best she could.

When she returned, his soft snore filled the room, and the tension in his back had relaxed. His injured arm hung over the edge of the bed and the small red stains in the bandage tugged at her. With no more arguments, she climbed under the covers, facing away from Hunter.

Heat from his close proximity bathed her with a strange comfort. Alessandra sighed, letting the exhaustion finally drag her under.

Chapter 4

HUNTER WOKE AND BLINKED at his surroundings. His shirt was balled up on the floor and his senses were back to their heightened wolf level. Alessandra's arm draped around his waist and he stared at it for a moment before turning his head.

The movement made her stir, and she pulled her arm with her as she rolled onto her back.

The absence of her skin against his almost pulled a groan from his throat. If she didn't address this attraction, he had to cut her loose for sanity's sake.

She made the sweetest noise and stretched. It took everything he had not to pounce, and he took a deep soothing breath to staunch the fire burning in his soul.

Alessandra's eyes popped open, and her head snapped in his direction. She nearly jumped from the bed, her gaze jumping from him to their surroundings. He could almost see the click in her mind as the memory of where they were, and why, flooded her brain. Red bloomed in her cheeks, and she rolled her shoulder.

It was amazing what solid rest did for a werewolf. His arm had the faint itch of healing. If he peeled back the gauze, there would be nothing but light scratches, and he ventured to guess Alessandra's shoulder was healed. He'd have to remove the stitches after they got out of here.

"You didn't yield," she said, and her hands found her waist.

Just like that, the serene morning turned to shit, and aggravation braised every inch of him. He climbed out of bed and swiped the shirt off the floor, passing by her without a word. When he finished his business and rinsed the sleep from his mouth, he opened the bathroom door.

Alessandra stood, shifting from foot to foot, and almost ran him down in her bid to get inside the washroom. Hunter straightened out the bed and cocked his head, listening for signs of life upstairs. Nothing stirred.

He rested his gaze on Alessandra when she stepped out of the bathroom and then headed up the stairs. He tried the doorknob and let out a small sigh of relief when it turned easily. The morning sun spilled into the living room and the note sitting on the nearest table caught his attention.

"They unlocked the door?" Alessandra said from behind him.

"Yes. And left a note. They went to get us some gas. They said to help ourselves in the kitchen." He held the note so she could see. "I guess he didn't want us alone with the kids," he added with a shrug.

"You didn't answer me downstairs," she said, returning to her scolding.

"I'm not yours to command, Ally. We had this discussion yesterday before the shooting started."

"Bullshit. I'm the alpha here."

Her domineering tone set him off, and he spun on his heel. "You really want to challenge me right now?" he barked.

"I want you to snap out of this shit. Now," she said.

"In all the years we've known each other, have you ever seen me just bow down to you because you told me to?" he asked.

"You always did what I asked."

He laughed. Miss high and mighty needed to be set in her place. "I did what was right for the pack, and most times that coincided with your requests. Jesus, do you really think I'd blindly follow anyone? Are you that fucking naïve?"

She glared at him.

"You don't know a goddamned thing about me, do you?" he snarled. "I bet you don't even know my real name?"

She blinked at him. "Hunter Blaez," she said meekly, and it burned right in the center of his core.

"No. It's actually Jacob. Jacob Randall Blaez. Hunter is a fucking nickname my dad gave me when I was younger, and it stuck." He towered over her, glaring down into her upturned face, torn between walking away and taking her in his arms.

"Well, I bet you don't know anything about me." She crossed her arms. Her lips pressed together in that smug way that sent him over the edge.

"Your name is Alessandra Elizabeth Tate," he said, with no hesitation and her eyes widened. "Your favorite color is blue, and your favorite food isn't steak, like it is for most wolves. It's actually spicy chicken. You talk to your dead mother every night before you go to sleep, asking her to guide you, and you curse your father for leaving you behind and taking the council's side. You pretend to hate chick flicks, but you secretly love them as much as you do action films. And while you flinch at the thought of a man touching you, deep down, you want someone to make that pain disappear. Do you need me to continue?"

Her eyes narrowed, and her jaw tightened. He stepped closer, and she backed into the wall. Hunter planted his hands on either side of her head and leaned forward so his eyes were level with hers.

"I'm also aware that you sense whatever the hell this is between us."

The sound of the garage door pulled him away, and he stepped into the kitchen, finding two coffee cups along with sugar and creamer waiting next to the pot. He poured both cups and fixed Alessandra's the way she liked it and left his black, hoping it was strong enough to fuel him for the day.

He turned and handed the cup to her, and she raised an eyebrow.

"I'm mad, not a dick," he mumbled as the door to the house opened.

"I see you found the coffee," Stan said as three teenagers bounded into the house. Two girls and a boy came in and the girls stopped short at the sight of him.

"We hear you got attacked by a bear," the boy said from behind the two stunned girls.

Hunter pulled his shirtsleeve up to show the bandage. "Yeah and I lived. Can you believe it?" He sent a grin their way and sent a side-eye at Alessandra. "Your dad was kind enough to help us out." He reached into his back pocket and pulled out his wallet. "How much do I owe you for the gas?"

Stan waved his hand. "Don't worry about it."

Hunter's senses prickled. Alessandra was too busy sipping her coffee to catch the nuance of fear from Stan. The kids headed down the hall and Stan watched them go before he turned back to Hunter.

"So..." Stan's eyes darted between Hunter and Alessandra.

Hunter put down his cup. "We should be going. We've taken up too much of your time and kindness already," he said. "Come on, honey," he said to Alessandra, and held his hand out.

Alessandra still clutched her coffee, and she stared at his offered hand for a second before she slid into character. She set the cup on the counter and slipped her hand in his. Hunter's chest loosened as she smiled at Stan.

"Thank you so much for your hospitality," she said.

"Why are your boots in the jeep?" Stan asked before they passed, and Hunter stopped.

He bit his lip and sighed. "Would you really have permitted us to come in if I had my boots on?" He waited, meeting Stan's gaze.

"It was my idea," Alessandra added. "We needed help, and Mr. Skeptical here said no one in their right mind would let us in their house that late at night."

Hunter raised an eyebrow at her, impressed at her improv skills.

Stan huffed. "So, why did you have shoes and she didn't?"

Hunter shifted and looked down at the ground. "I was getting a little too close to nature," he said, and smirked. "And she struck back."

Stan pressed his lips together. "Really?" Sarcasm laced the question.

"I didn't realize a mamma bear was hibernating in the brush I relieved myself in." He shifted, wondering if they should have chosen some other animal. It was rare for bears to be out and about at this time of year, and if he had been thinking straight, he might have chosen something else, instead of a bear attack.

Stan reached out and grabbed the rifle leaning on the wall. "You sure it has nothing to do with that home invasion a couple of towns over?" He turned his phone towards them, and their pictures graced the screen with a wanted sign underneath.

Shit. "Yes." Hunter said as he moved his gaze from his picture to Stan. "My arm wasn't torn to shreds by a person."

Alessandra squeezed his hand. "That was our house," she said, drawing Stan's attention. "Someone attacked us."

"This says there's an outstanding warrant for your arrest." He waved his phone at them.

Hunter pulled the side of his lip between his teeth. The gun wasn't quite level, but Stan had his fingers near enough to the trigger to keep Hunter from trying to rip the weapon from him.

Noises behind them caused Alessandra's hand to clamp down on his.

"We didn't come here for trouble," Hunter said softly. "We needed some rest, and now we'll get out of your hair."

The cock of a gun behind them made him close his eyes.

"You really don't want to do this." Hunter met Stan's gaze.

"Why not?"

Hunter took a gamble. "If someone you loved was raped and beaten and left for dead, what would you do?"

The gun lowered, and Stan's jaw tightened.

"I took justice into my own hands. That's why I have an outstanding warrant."

Alessandra's head lowered and her shame and horror swept over him. He gave her hand a squeeze, glad she still held tight.

"And some son of a bitch bounty hunter shot us out of our home last night."

"Your arm?" he asked, pointing the barrel of the gun.

"To be honest, I'm clueless about what happened," he confessed because he had run out of lies. "I didn't even know I was bleeding until we pulled into your driveway." He sighed.

"Please, just let us go," Alessandra said. "We really don't want any trouble."

"What about the reward, Pa?" the boy behind them said.

Her hand tightened around Hunter's, as if she had an inkling of the question that would be asked next.

"Is he telling the truth about what happened to you?"

Hunter glanced at her, and the shame was visible in the heightened color of her cheeks, but the single tear that escaped her right eye said more than her slight nod. It broke his heart, and he took a deep breath, blinking back the wetness in his own eyes.

Stan seemed to be affected in the same manner. The barrel of the shotgun dropped to the floor. He looked beyond them to the boy. "I understand you wanted that reward, son, but I can't, in good conscience, hold these two."

"They could be lying," he said, and both Alessandra and Hunter turned to look at him.

The boy's gaze moved from Hunter to Alessandra. The gun slowly lowered. Somehow, he could see the damage reflected in her eyes, and relief washed over Hunter. He let out the breath he wasn't aware he had been holding.

With no more words, he led Alessandra out the front door.

Alessandra took the driver's seat, moving his boots to the back seat. "I'm driving," she said. "Want to put the gas they got into the tank?"

Hunter peered at the gas can on the ground near the entrance. His feet were already cold, but he could deal with the snow biting his flesh for a few more minutes. He grabbed the container and emptied the contents into the Jeep's gas tank. Before jumping into the car, he put the empty container back where he'd found it and then slid into the passenger seat.

Alessandra had the heater going, and the flow of warm air on his cold feet felt good.

"Where to?" she asked.

Hunter digested the question as she pulled to the end of the driveway. Heading back in the direction they came would most likely be a death sentence.

"North and West is really where I want to go, but there is no way we can cross the border with our faces plastered all over the news." The

Canadian border was less than a two-hour drive from their current hiding place in central Maine. "It's also the direction they will assume we've gone since they tracked us here."

"Then we go the opposite direction."

"We can't go much farther East, honey," he said, glancing at her.

Her lips pressed together, and she shot him a glare.

He couldn't suppress his grin fast enough, and looked out the window instead. "Where do you think the last place they'd look for us would be?"

"The Florida Keys," she said.

He laughed. Werewolves were not known for their fondness of heat, and the Keys were the last place he wanted to go. Just the thought brought sweat to the surface, and he wiped his neck, shuddering at the thought. It also meant no hunting grounds. They'd have to actually work to buy food in order to survive.

"The only other place hotter is probably Arizona," he said. At least the desert would give them a chance to hunt.

"Yeah, but they'll look there. They won't look at the islands, where we can't hunt."

Hunter sighed and gave a nod. "The Florida Keys it is."

Chapter 5

ALESSANDRA'S EYELIDS DROOPED AND her right leg ached. She had been driving a little over twelve hours, and the Washington, DC traffic had nearly done her in. Hunter slumped in the passenger seat. He had slept most of the drive. The lack of conversation between them wasn't exactly ideal, but at least he hadn't brought up the argument from this morning.

She had only stopped for gas, paying cash from Hunter's stash. And at each stop, he woke and asked if she'd like him to drive. She had needed to concentrate on the road, otherwise all the thoughts and feelings bottled inside her would overflow, and she had no idea what that would bring.

"You need to let me drive."

She startled when she heard his voice and the car swerved, narrowly missing the truck in the next lane.

"Jesus!" she snapped, as her heart pounded in her throat. That pleasant lull of hypnotic driving had disappeared at the sound of his voice.

"Why don't we get off at the next exit, grab some food, and then I can drive for the next stretch," he said, in that perfectly reasonable tone that made her want to growl at him, despite her stomach being in full agreement.

"Fine," she said.

He raised his eyebrow at her. "You're the one who insisted on driving," he said, picking up on her irritation.

Alessandra took a deep breath. He was right. Her foul mood really had more to do with her internal reflection over the last twelve hours.

"Maybe we should find a place to sleep for the night." She didn't want to sleep in the passenger seat. While Hunter could drop to sleep almost anywhere, she could never sleep soundly in a car.

"I'll be good to drive for a while."

"I need a bed, not an uncomfortable bucket seat."

He raised an eyebrow. "I slept just fine."

"You could sleep anywhere. I can't."

"Fine," he said, and shifted in the seat. "We can find somewhere off the next exit. If we're going to just hang out for the night, I may go out for a bit."

"Why?" she asked, giving him a sideways glance.

"Once I fully wake up and eat, I'm not going to be able to fall asleep right away. Not after sleeping for this long. I'll have too much energy and I'll need to burn some of it off."

"How?" she asked, keeping her eyes peeled for an exit sign.

"I don't know. Maybe I'll go for a run. Or maybe I'll find a bar and get drunk."

She snapped her head in his direction and the grin that he tried to hide surfaced. He was needling her on purpose.

"Fuck you," she muttered.

"That's another way I can release some energy," he said.

"Stop it." This obviously was the end of her peaceful drive.

"We need to finish our conversation from this morning," he said, and stretched in the passenger seat.

All things considered, Alessandra had ended up with a protector who was very easy on the eyes. She shook her head, trying to clear that thought from her mind.

"Was that a no?"

His voice carried a challenge she wasn't prepared to face. She also wasn't ready to deal with the truth of his words this morning. She'd had a long drive with him sleeping. A long time to think about the chemistry that had always seemed to exist. She just mistook it as some strange brotherly-type over-protectiveness.

Hell, he had dated, even flaunted his girls to the pack. She had always been highly skeptical of the women he brought to meet them. None of them were ever good enough for him. Not in her mind, and now that she looked back, it seemed to stem more from jealousy than her alpha scrutiny.

She had dated as well, and he had been just as critical of the guys she'd introduced to the pack. Jeremy was a gross misjudgment, and Alessandra was sure if she had introduced him to her pack, they would have picked up on his dark intentions. Jeremy had stripped her of any trust of the male population, including Hunter.

She wasn't sure she'd ever find that trust again, despite any attraction that might be there under the surface.

Instead of answering his question, she took the next exit and followed the lodging signs. She pulled into a seedy-looking motel on the main strip, and grinned at the sign.

The Hunter Motel in Newington, Virginia, certainly wasn't the type of hotel she would normally stay at, but it had a little restaurant attached, and it was the only place visible on the strip.

Hunter's dimples appeared when she pulled up next to the office. He went to step out of the jeep.

"Maybe I should go in," she said. "You look the same as your wanted poster."

"And you don't?"

"No. Not like you do." Alessandra took her long hair and rolled it into a bun. Hunter raised an eyebrow at her when her lips curved up at the corners in a sly smirk. She scanned her reflection in the mirror and secured the tight bun. With her hair pulled away from her face, she looked less like the girl in the poster.

"I'll be right back." She grabbed a handful of bills from the box hidden in the console.

She strode into the office and stifled a yawn with her hand. A pimply guy sat at the desk, gaping at something she couldn't see. She cleared her throat, and he jumped.

"I need a room for the night. Preferably ground floor near the restaurant, if possible," she asked.

"The only one I have on the first floor near the restaurant has a single king. Is that okay?" he asked, as he pushed aside whatever had captivated him.

As much as she would prefer separate beds, the location of the room was more important. "That's fine."

With the key in hand, she slid back into the jeep. She studied Hunter's beard and shoulder-length hair. He looked exactly like the wanted poster, and she had never seen him without scruff on his face or a short haircut.

"You need to change your look." She speared a look in his direction as she pulled into the parking space in front of their room.

"What's wrong with my look?" He sent her a sideways glance before he slipped out and opened the back.

She waited at the door while Hunter grabbed the oversized suitcase. He followed her inside, and she closed the door before he could comment on the accommodations.

He set the suitcase down on the dresser and flipped it open. "I need a shower before we eat." He didn't even peek in her direction; instead, he grabbed clothes out of the suitcase and disappeared into the bathroom.

She needed to clean up as well and stepped to the bag to see what he'd packed in their emergency exit kit. She retrieved a sundress and spaghetti strap sandals, smiling. It wasn't quite warm enough in Virginia, but Florida would be perfect for this. Jeans, shorts and t-shirts were the only other things left in the suitcase, along with nightclothes. She pulled out a second pair of jeans and a plain blue t-shirt that matched Hunter's eyes. He had packed underwear and a couple of bras for her as well. His stash was mostly the same. Jeans and t-shirts, but under it all, he'd also packed a suit and dress shoes. The dichotomy of the different clothing tickled her.

She climbed on the bed and switched the television on while she waited. Another yawn caught her off guard, especially with the accompanying stomach rumble. The shower had gone off a while ago and Alessandra wondered what the hell he was doing in there. She needed food and sleep, and if he didn't come out soon, she was going to march in there and take over the bathroom.

She stood up to do just that when the door opened. The man standing there didn't look at all familiar. His short, dark locks were slicked back, and his clean-shaven cheeks glowed in the dim light. His bright blue eyes sparkled under the frame of deep black lashes. He was stunningly handsome.

"Hunter?" she couldn't help but ask.

His teeth shone pearly through his grin. "Better?" He waved at his face.

"Holy shit," she said, and before she could stop herself, she crossed and ran her hand down his cheek. It was as smooth as she imagined it would be.

He captured her hand, holding it in place as he stared down at her. "I gather you like the new look?"

The heat from his breath tickled her wrist, and she pulled it from his grip.

"I may have ruined your razor, though," he said as she slipped past him.

She closed the bathroom door and leaned on it, trying to catch her breath. She had never seen him clean shaven. Nor had she ever seen him with short hair. With long hair and a beard, he looked more like a free-spirited hippie, but with what he looked like now, he could easily walk into a modeling agency in New York and be given a contract on the spot.

Her gaze landed on the sink and the stray hairs he had missed in his attempt to clean up. The scissors from the first aid kit sat on the edge of the sink, along with her razor. She huffed a laugh, hoping the razor had a little sharpness left, but she doubted it.

She undressed and peeled off the bandages on her shoulder. The bullet hole was gone, but the stitches were still there. Alessandra wrapped a towel around herself and opened the door.

"Did you want to take these out before I jump in the shower?"

Hunter's gaze jumped from the stitches to the towel wrapped around her before he gave a nod and climbed off the bed. He took a seat on the closed toilet and grabbed the scissors from the sink before pulling her close.

"And you couldn't do this because?" he asked as he snipped each stitch.

"Because it freaks me out a little." She met his gaze and then looked at the ceiling. The pull on her skin sent a chill through her and she shivered.

He shifted her closer and continued to remove each thread. When he finished, his hands landed on her waist, pulling her gaze from the ceiling to his. Warmth radiated through her.

"All done," he said, but he stayed put and she didn't move from between his knees.

The moment stretched as she searched his eyes. There was no denying the attraction that lived between them, but it terrified her. His hand cupped her cheek and the fondness that filled his eyes brought a lump to her throat.

"Do you feel it?" he whispered with such desperation that her heart ached.

She leaned into his hand, unable to say yes, and unable to deny the electricity flowing through her entire form. He slid forward and pressed his lips to hers. The soft contact set her heart on overdrive and broke through her paralysis.

She stepped away, grasping at the towel to keep it in place. Hunter leaned back and took a deep breath before the hardness returned to his features.

"Clean up. I need food just as much as you do," he said, and left the bathroom, slamming the door behind him.

Alessandra stepped into the shower and dialed it to the coldest setting her skin would allow, staunching the heat that had encompassed her the moment Hunter's lips found hers.

Chapter 6

HUNTER SAT ON THE edge of the bed listening to the water run. His heart still hammered in his chest. Alessandra hadn't flinched. She had actually kissed back for a moment before she stepped away. The woman hadn't refused to acknowledge the presence of something, so all his posturing at Stan's house must have sunk in.

He glanced at the door and sighed, running his hand through his short hair. The whole situation left his nerves raw and his libido chomping at the bit. The beast in him wanted to storm in and take her to heights she'd never experienced, but the man kept him in check. If he gave in to his animal instincts, that would ruin everything.

As much as she infuriated him, he longed to break through her barriers. He yearned to be the one who fixed her. He wished to be the one to erase the nightmares. The truth of being in love with Alessandra had always been rough, but now that she was aware, she was seeing him as a man and not her backup wolf.

The door finally opened, and she stepped out. Her wet hair hung loosely around her face, and she avoided his gaze.

"We need to figure out what to call each other."

Her gaze snapped to his. "What do you mean?"

"Well, with the outstanding warrants looking for Hunter Blaez and Alessandra Tate, we should probably start calling each other something different in public."

Her arms crossed. "Why didn't they use your real name?"

"Because the dipshits don't know it. I've got my original birth certificate and my social security number with me. My driver's license was mistakenly made using my nickname, and I never corrected it. Because of that, all my credit cards and loans and shit were made out to Hunter Blaez."

Her eyebrows went up.

"Yeah. My father decided I should leave it alone, and he made sure I had my documents before he died. He said to keep them close in case I needed to make a run for it. I guess he was aware that I'd get myself in trouble someday."

"But how did you figure out to take them with you?"

Hunter chuckled. "My dad never trusted the council, and he taught me to be prepared for anything. Why do you think I have a hidden compartment in my car?"

Alessandra studied him. "It's like you're a complete stranger to me."

"I'm a survivalist, Ally. And I had the forethought to grab my personal shit before I left my house that night." He laughed. "I remember second guessing myself, trying to laugh away the urgency in the pit of my stomach. But I still listened. I still packed up my father's fortune and anything that would do me any good on the road. When I left the house that night, I knew I was never going back home." He paused and closed his eyes. "I'm not sure if it was the wolf thing between us, or if it was some kind of warning from my father, but my heart was in my throat that entire night. The pack wasn't all that cooperative, either. They just wanted to go hunting and have some fun, but I couldn't. I said we needed to track you down, especially when I couldn't get hold of you on your cell. They thought I was fucking nuts until we caught your scent in those woods."

"I didn't know," she whispered, and crossed to the suitcase, depositing her dirty clothing on the side.

He stood and stepped behind her, looking at her reflection. "At least you have something to call me." Her lips twitched into a smirk, and she met his gaze in the mirror. "And it's not asshole."

"Aww. I kind of like that," she whined, pulling a grin to his face.

"Seriously. What do you want me to call you? Sandra?"

She wrinkled her nose in response and then chewed her bottom lip. Just the motion of her lip sliding into her mouth distracted him. "How about Leigh?" she asked.

His eyebrows went up as he considered it. Instead of reacting to the visceral need to kiss her, he concentrated on the name, framing it in his mind and silently saying it in his head.

"I actually like that," he said, and she turned towards him, looking up into his eyes.

"I'm glad," she said, and licked her lips. "Jake."

"Jacob," he said, correcting her. He wanted her to call him by his rightful name, not another nickname.

"Jake," she repeated, challenging him.

He rolled his eyes. "Fine. You ready to go grab some food, Leigh?" He had mixed feelings about her new nickname for him, but he certainly liked the way Leigh rolled off his tongue. From the pink hue in her cheeks, she seemed to like it as well.

They were seated at the little diner, and he looked over the menu. The bacon cheeseburger looked like it would hit the spot, and he closed his menu. Alessandra had her hands folded neatly over the menu and she was fixated on the moving traffic out the window.

"Leigh, we need to talk about earlier," he said, figuring the restaurant was a safe space, one that neither of them would make a scene in.

She blinked at him, pointing her finger at her chest in such a way that Hunter wanted to drag her from the restaurant and put her over his knee. He clenched his teeth.

"This is not the place," she said, eyeing the approaching hostess.

Hunter turned his attention to the perky waitress, leveling the sizzling smile he had been told would make Mother Teresa take him to bed. The waitress reacted, smiling back and nearly ignoring Alessandra. Out of the corner of his eye, he saw her bristle. If she had been in wolf form, all her hair would be standing on end and her teeth would be bared. Hunter couldn't help it. The jealousy radiating from her stroked his ego in a way it hadn't been stroked in years.

"What can I getcha?" the waitress asked, her sole focus on Hunter.

"My girlfriend will have a spicy chicken sandwich with fries and a vanilla milkshake."

At the mention of girlfriend, the waitress' leer faltered.

"And I'll have three bacon cheeseburgers, along with a vanilla milkshake."

The waitress wandered away with their order, and he focused back on Alessandra.

"Girlfriend?"

"It's better than alpha bitch."

Her eyes narrowed.

"I have half a mind to kick your ass," she muttered under her breath. It wasn't quite low enough for him not to pick it up.

"Maybe we can do that when we get back to the room," he teased, in the same low tone.

Her lips twitched up at the edges, and for the first time in a very long time, her eyes sparkled with mirth.

The waitress came with their vanilla milkshakes, and she gave a tight facsimile of a smile to the two of them and dropped the straws in the middle of the table. Hunter waited until she was out of hearing range before picking up the straws and offering one to Alessandra.

"Aren't you tired of pretending?" he asked, after he took a sip.

The shine in her eyes dulled. He silently kicked himself.

"I haven't been."

All his good humor disappeared. "What do you want to do when we get to Key West?" he asked, changing the subject because her denial was just as infuriating as her cluelessness had been. There was no use in arguing in the restaurant.

"Swim in the ocean," she said.

"I was thinking about getting a boat. Maybe a cabin cruiser." He sent her a sideways glance.

"Don't you need a boating license?"

He leaned closer. "Jacob has one in his name." He met her gaze and leaned back, relishing her open-mouthed stare. He had played shadow, and then nursemaid, for way too long. It was time to peel back the layers of who he really was. It might be a risk, but everything they did now was a risk.

"As I said before, I don't know a thing about you."

He grinned and took a sip of his milkshake. "The key question here is, do you, or do you not, want to find out what truly makes me tick?" He challenged her with a raise of his eyebrow.

Blush crawled through her cheeks, and she couldn't meet his gaze. The waitress came with their food, and he swore she exhaled with relief. Instead of focusing on her, his mind, as well as his stomach, pulled to the plate in front of him. A small voice in the back of his head reminded him to mind his manners. He was in a public venue, not in the middle of the woods devouring a fresh kill.

Alessandra must have been thinking the same, because they ate like civilized adults. When the plates were cleared, and the meal done, he wiped his mouth with a napkin and met her gaze.

"I'm going to have to go on a run after this," he said.

"I need sleep." She covered the yawn that followed.

"You don't want to go for a short run?"

She shook her head.

After peeling off enough cash to cover the bill and a decent tip, they left the restaurant and headed back to the room. Stepping inside, he closed the shades and locked the door, before sitting in the chair near the table, while she changed in the bathroom. His light mood at the restaurant had darkened. He didn't want to leave her alone in the hotel room, but he needed to get rid of this pent-up energy inside him. His fingers drummed on the table while his knee bounced.

Alessandra stepped out of the bathroom and his entire form went still. She wore a spaghetti strapped nightshirt that came down to her mid-thigh. The sweetheart neckline showed some of her cleavage. He'd completely forgotten he had thrown that in the suitcase and seeing it on her turned the fire inside him into an inferno.

He stood to leave.

"Please don't go."

He stopped with his hand on the chain, fully aware that his body had reacted to the sexiness of the outfit along with the plea in her voice.

"Ally, you really don't want me to stay."

Silence filled the space long enough for him to look over his shoulder. The way she hugged herself and stared at the ground clawed at him and he sighed.

"You really think I'm a bitch?" Her gaze lifted, but this time, there was a feral challenge in her eyes.

He turned to face her. "So, you really want to kick my ass?" He crossed the distance and stared down at her. "Go for it," he whispered, sensing the beast bristling within him.

Without any warning, he was suddenly on his back on the ground with Alessandra straddling him. She also had his wrists pinned to the ground on either side of his head. The growl in the back of her throat was the sexiest thing he had ever heard, and his body responded. He ambushed her with a smile.

She blinked down at him. "You're not supposed to be enjoying this," she snapped.

"I disagree." He rolled, pinning her underneath him, using her grip against her. He stared down at her. His smirk faded at the fear now present in her eyes. "I'm not going to do anything," he breathed, and rose to his knees, letting her scuttle out from underneath him.

Her breath remained ragged as she sat on the corner of the bed. He climbed to his feet and took the space next to her. The mattress vibrated. Alessandra's entire body trembled, and her hair blocked her face.

Hunter reached out and tucked the strands behind her ear. This time, she flinched away from him.

"Fuck," he growled, and sprung to his feet. A silver knife slicing through his abdomen would have been a lot less painful. He headed straight towards the door.

"Jacob," her shaking voice stopped him, along with the use of his real name.

"What?" His heart squeezed with disappointment and a level of fury he could hardly contain. If he could turn the clock back, he would relish every scream and dying gurgle that came out of those bastards.

"I'm afraid," she whispered.

"Of what?"

"Of everything."

He leaned his head against the door and asked the only question that really mattered. "Do you ever think you could love me?"

"Yes," the softest whisper reached his ears, and he turned, meeting her tear-stained eyes. "But I'm not sure I will ever trust anyone again."

A part of him growled inside. He was uncertain about what else he could do to earn her trust. Instead of heading out for a much-needed run, he collapsed in the chair next to the door. He would not get any relief from the pent-up emotions locked inside him. What he really wanted to do was rip that negligee off her and lick every inch of her skin.

Alessandra just stared at him. "What's going through your mind?"

He huffed a laugh. "You really want to know?" he asked.

She slid under the covers, pulling the sheet up to her chin. She looked like a terrified child, and he cursed the want pulsing in his blood.

"Honestly?"

She gave a single nod.

"I was just thinking about licking every inch of your skin."

Her eyes widened and her cheeks turned bright pink.

"You asked."

She let out a nervous laugh and her gaze found the ceiling.

"But I'll stay right here for the night because the thought freaks you out."

The red in her cheeks blotched and tears slipped from the corner of her eyes.

He leaned his head back and stared at the ceiling. His hands gripped the arms of the chairs so hard the metal under the fabric groaned. "Someday, I'd like to be the one to replace those nightmares with something tender and loving."

"I have nightmares it's you hurting me," she said, through a hitched breath. "Those are the ones that undo me every time."

His gaze found hers and it took every ounce of willpower not to cross the room and take her in his arms. Every detail of her pain scraped at him and he pressed his lips together, blinking away the mist that covered his eyes.

"No one is going to hurt you like that ever again," he said. "Not while I'm breathing."

When she held her arms out for him, he scrambled across the distance and pulled her into his chest. Her sobs shook her form, and he stroked her silky hair, softly cooing in her ears until her last hitching breaths wound down.

"On a lighter note, at least you didn't vomit when I kissed you earlier."

Her halfhearted laugh brought a spark of hope to his heart. She pulled away, and he met her gaze, wiping the tears from her cheeks with his thumbs. A tear came to rest at the corner of her mouth and before she could catch it with her tongue, Hunter leaned in and delivered a kiss that caught the tear.

She gasped, and the opportunity presented itself. He slid his tongue into her mouth, exploring. Alessandra stiffened under his lips, but her tongue tentatively swiped his, slowly rolling in a sensual circle. He groaned with the sweetness of it.

She planted her hand on his chest and the kiss deepened right before she pushed him away. He met her gaze, and they stared at each other for what seemed an eternity. For the first time, he saw the spark of want in her eyes, but alongside it was her fear.

He planted a kiss on her forehead and headed into the bathroom, locking the door behind him. As he stripped his clothes, he debated between a cold shower or satisfying his need for release. He didn't think a cold shower would do anything to quell the pent-up energy in the center of his being. So, he dialed the water to hot and stepped under the spray. With his hand soaped up, he closed his eyes and imagined all the decadent things he wanted to do to Alessandra.

He sped his stroke as the energy pooled in his belly. In his mind's eye, Alessandra moved under him with the same fervor, her hips rising to meet his. He clenched his mouth closed and squeezed his eyes tight as his body responded. He kept stroking, his body jerking with the force of each spurt. He slowed his stroke and opened his eyes. His jizz dripped from the wall and he let out a light chuckle at how much had come out. It had been way too long since he'd had any form of release. Hunter cleaned both himself and the shower walls and then dialed the water into the frigid zone to cool the heat still burning inside.

By the time he stepped into the bedroom, he had his libido in check. Alessandra's soft breathing told him she was sound asleep, and he sighed and changed into a pair of running shorts. Halfway to the door, her soft groan stopped him. The acrid stench of fear spread through the room.

Her moan became a muffled scream, and he closed his eyes, turning around and stepping close to the bed. Gently, he ran his fingers through her hair, starting at her temple.

"It's okay, baby," he whispered. "It's okay."

"No!"

Her scream shot to the depths of his soul, and she shot up to a sitting position, panting. Her eyes darted around frantically, finally landing on him kneeling by the side of the bed.

"You died." Her voice shook. "They found us and I watched you die."

Hunter sat on the edge of the bed facing her. "It was just a dream," he said, trying to keep his voice soft and calm, like he always did when she had nightmares. Although the subject of this one differed from the others. Usually, her nightmares revolved around the horrors that happened to her in the fraternity van.

Her arms encircled his neck, shocking him into momentary inaction. When his brain caught up, his arms wrapped around her as tightly as hers were around his neck. Her trembling turned his nerves into raw receptors, and he pressed his lips to the edge of her throat, nuzzling her neck. His fingers grazed the sides of her breasts. "It was just a dream," he whispered in her ear, but held fast, not wanting this intimate moment to end.

Her trembling subsided, but her grip on him didn't loosen. Instead, her lips found the side of his neck. Her butterfly kisses nearly made him lose all the control the cold shower had given him.

"Don't start something you have no intent on finishing," he warned, and her teeth clamped down on his earlobe. Chills rippled through him and his grip tightened. "Ally, please," he whispered. He wasn't sure if he was asking her to stop or asking for permission to ravage her.

"I need you."

Her whisper tickled his ear. He pulled her away, making her meet his gaze. "This isn't what you want," he said. Her fear still radiated like a poison in the air.

"I need this," she said, and her eyes filled with tears.

"What do you need?" he asked, making sure he understood her clearly. An assumption right now would kill their entire future.

"You. I need you to make the nightmares go away." She wrapped her hand around to the back of his head and pulled him to her lips.

The urgency in her kiss erased any logic from his mind and before he had any awareness, he had laid her back on the bed and his hand had already traveled under the hem of her nightshirt. His lips moved from hers to the v between her breasts. She arched into it, letting out a purr that shot his heart into his stomach. He peeled her shoulder straps down her arms and pushed the fabric of the night shirt below her breasts, taking a moment to caress each one before he lowered his mouth to her nipples.

Her fear remained, but mingled with the scent was yearning, and he continued caressing and kissing her skin. When he sat up to pull her shirt the rest of the way off, her entire body went rigid. He stared at her, at her clamped eyes. He thought twice about removing her underwear. Instead, he lowered his mouth to her stomach, licking a path from one side to the other.

Gooseflesh rolled across the path he'd just kissed. The closer he got to her underwear, the tenser she became. While he just wanted to bury his face between her legs, he avoided that for now. Instead, he kissed his way down each of her thighs.

When he reached the top of her feet, she had relaxed enough to seem to enjoy his pampering. He met her gaze. "Roll onto your stomach," he said, and alarm flashed in her eyes. "Trust me," he whispered, and took her toe in his mouth, sucking it gently before relinquishing it. He knew how hard those two words were for her and he remained in place, massaging her foot while he waited for her to comply. If she didn't, the exploration would be over for tonight, and every cell in his body did not want this to end.

He kept eye contact and when she rolled onto her stomach and looked over her shoulder, he just sent a ghost of a smile her way. The mistrust in her eyes, along with the mix of emotions in her scent, held him in place for a moment.

ALESSANDRA STARED INTO HIS sparkling blue eyes, wondering if trusting him would be a mistake. But the sincerity in his gaze told her otherwise. Her entire body throbbed with adrenaline and desire, but the thin veil of fear covering her held her back from truly enjoying Hunter's touch.

He closed his eyes and brought the foot he had been massaging to his lips, running his tongue down her arch. Her foot tingled from the contact, spiraling up her leg right to her core. She bit her lip against the moan and curled her arms around the pillow, resting her cheek on the soft fabric.

When he moved to her ankle, she moaned at the sensations his mouth and tongue created. His hands were gentle as they kneaded her calves, melting away the tension. As his hands and mouth drew close to her ass, the tension returned, but this time, it was in anticipation of his touch, not dread.

Her breath hitched when his tongue followed the line of her panties. His hands continued to massage the back of her thighs and all she wanted was for him to slide them between her legs and massage her clit. Hunter's touch was intoxicating, and his avoidance of the only area clad in fabric was driving her mad.

By the time he got to her neck, she was genuinely panting with need and shuddering with every swipe of his tongue.

"Roll onto your back," he whispered.

This time there was no hesitation, and when his mouth traveled from her shoulder to her hand, she closed her eyes, silently willing him to travel lower again. When he sucked her index finger into his mouth, she opened her eyes. Every muscle trembled when he straddled her and a measure of disappointment laced her stomach when he took her other hand, exploring her with his mouth.

He followed the line of her arm to her neck before planting a kiss on her lips. Hunter pulled away and stared down at her. "I think that's enough for one night," he said. His voice was huskier than she'd ever heard it.

Alessandra whined. She couldn't voice what she wanted, but she pleaded with her eyes, praying he could read her as deeply as he professed.

His slow smile sent a shiver up her spine. "You have to say the words, Leigh," he said, and the use of the new name they'd agreed on did something to her insides she didn't understand. Warmth flowed through her.

Alessandra licked her lips. "Please, don't stop," she said. Her voice trembled.

He lowered his mouth to her breasts, sucking the hard nubs until she moaned. He moved lower in as slow a progression as before. His tongue traced her stomach along the edge of her underwear. His legs still straddled her, although he had moved down over her knees.

Hunter slowly looked up, meeting her gaze as his hand slid between her thighs. His thumb slowly circled over her clit, creating an inferno inside her. Alessandra pulled her legs out from between his and spread them wide, almost ensnaring him with her limbs. Her intent was as clear as she could make it without words.

Hunter's breath caught in his chest. The want in his eyes was as all-consuming as his touch.

"Are you sure?" he asked, even while his thumb kept circling.

"You wanted to lick every inch of me," she said, empowered by the heat consuming her.

Hunter groaned in response and the ripping of fabric followed. He dropped between her legs, even as his thumb kept that insane circling. He licked the inside of her thigh, and then the other, teasing, circling everywhere but where she wanted him.

When his mouth replaced his thumb, Alessandra sighed. "Jacob," she whispered, because somehow that was more fitting of the moment. The sensation of his name rolling off her tongue nearly matched the pleasure of his mouth playing with her clit.

Every motion of his mouth, every swipe of his tongue, brought her closer to letting go. Her heart slammed against the wall of her chest, her toes curled as the heat built inside her core. She grasped at the sheets, balling them up in her hands. When the wave crashed, she screamed with it, cum shooting out of her like a geyser.

Hunter's fingers slid inside her as he leaned back on his heels. His free hand disappeared inside his shorts, stroking with the same urgency as his fingers plunging inside her.

"Jesus fucking Christ," he groaned, squeezing his eyes shut and shuddering.

His hand slowed and then stilled inside her and he opened his eyes, meeting her gaze. Both of their breaths huffed, and she marveled at the magic he had just created. Alessandra had never had a true orgasm before and the old adages of it being an earth moving experience weren't exaggerated.

"I'm sorry. I got a little carried away," he said, removing his hand from between her legs. He grabbed his discarded shirt and wiped the hand that had been down his shorts before stretching out next to her.

She just stared at the ceiling, still too stunned at what had transpired to speak.

He rolled onto his side and propped his head up on his hand. "Are you mad?"

His question pulled her gaze to his. She shook her head and his lips curved into that devilish grin that sent a shiver down her spine.

"Just speechless?" he asked.

"Yeah." She kept his gaze. Her muscles were the consistency of an overcooked noodle, and she forced herself to raise her hand, cupping his cheek. She ran her thumb along the smooth cheekbone before she traced his lips with it.

Hunter sucked the tip between his teeth before just kissing the pad.

"Jacob," she whispered.

"Leigh," he replied, and rolled his eyes. "It really is weird calling you something other than Ally."

"I like it better than my real name. Either that, or it's just the way you say it that I like better."

"I gotta admit. Hearing my given name from your lips turns me on something fierce." His cheeks turned red.

As the limpness faded from her muscles, they ached with exhaustion. She reached down, grabbed her discarded nightgown, and slipped it on before curling into a ball on her side. Hunter's hand idly traced her back, and her eyes refused to remain open.

Chapter 7

HUNTER SLOWLY TRACED HER back for a long time, long after she fell asleep. Guilt bit at him yet again, and he wondered if everything that had happened to them was his fault. The slow cadence of his fingers across her skin did nothing to soothe his unease, and when he was certain she wouldn't wake, he climbed out of bed and straightened the covers before heading into the bathroom.

He splashed cold water on his face and brushed his teeth before staring at his reflection. "What were you thinking?"

Of course, his brain had not been the one in control, so thinking had nothing to do with any of it. Although he had to give himself a little credit. He'd refrained from making love to her like he wanted to. Instead, he purged that need with his hand. Again.

"I just hope she doesn't have any regrets in the morning," he mumbled, and headed back to the bed.

He crawled on top of the blankets and stretched on his back, tucking his hands behind his head. Hunter contemplated turning on the television until Alessandra rolled into the crook of his arm. He stared down at her. The peace in her features drew a smile to his lips, and he wrapped his arm around her, nuzzling into her hair.

Hunter thought back to the day he met Alessandra. He was thirteen and had gone hunting with his father. They were stalking a deer and before he had a chance to take off after his prey, an arrow pierced the ground in front of him, stopping him in his tracks. The shock shifted him back to human form, and he looked up into the tree behind him. Lying on the branch was a cute girl who was probably half his age.

"Mine," she hissed, and refocused on the deer. A second arrow flew true, and the deer dropped.

"That was our meal," Hunter said as she climbed down.

She gave him a cockeyed tilt of her mouth. "Go ahead. I'm sure my parents have something for me at home."

Even back then, the alpha in her was as apparent as her dark hair. He could also sense that she didn't seem to want the role. At least, not the way the other alphas projected it. He had seen his fair share of alphas, and none of them had ever given up a kill, not without a fight. She was different, and he knew at that moment he would gladly stand beside her and protect her from the bad in the world.

He was also aware she would likely be the death of him.

He closed his eyes, kissed the back of her head, and took a deep inhale, reveling in her sweet scent, drifting off into a satiated sleep.

SUNSHINE BROKE THROUGH THE crack in the curtain, shining right in her eye. She blinked and then lowered her gaze to the arms wrapped around her. Hunter's soft snore tickled her neck. She couldn't budge. He had her pinned by the blankets. Every muscle in her body tightened, and the air refused to fill her lungs.

The flood of memories of what his mouth and hands were capable of sent a shiver through her. In the light of day, the decisions she'd made last night didn't seem real.

"Hunter," she whispered, and the man shot up to a sitting position like someone had zapped him.

His gaze bounced around the room while his brain caught up to where he was. When his gaze dropped to hers, his mouth formed a crooked smile.

"Good morning," he said.

"Leave after breakfast?" she asked, rolling onto her back.

"Sounds good," he said, and slipped out of bed. He made a beeline right for the bathroom and Alessandra sighed, sitting up. Her gaze fell on her torn underwear lying in the middle of the carpet and heat filled her cheeks.

She crossed to the suitcase and filtered through the pile. If they traveled the same distance today, they'd be in Florida before the night was over, so she grabbed the sundress instead of jeans or shorts.

Hunter came out a few minutes later with a towel around his waist, smelling like fresh soap. Her gaze lingered for a moment before she stepped inside for a quick shower.

By the time she finished, Hunter had the suitcase closed and was ready to go. His eyes sparkled as they scanned her from head to toe.

"What am I supposed to do with this?" she held out her nightshirt and the small toiletry bag that held her razor and brushes. He stuffed the night shirt and bag into a side pocket before zipping it up.

"We have everything?" he asked, glancing around the room.

Both their gazes fell on the discarded underwear and then snapped to each other. His lips pressed together, trying to hide a grin, and her cheeks heated.

"Should we just leave it there?" Alessandra said, and Hunter's eyebrows arched. He opened his mouth to answer and then grinned.

"You are naughtier than I expected," he finally said.

"Perhaps you've awakened a beast," she said, and crossed to the door, swinging it open. A bolt of electricity hit the center of her chest and she froze in the doorway. She licked her lips and refused to look away from the dozen guns aimed at their hotel room door.

"Jake?"

He stood less than an inch behind her in the same state of shock she was in. His scent didn't alter as he scanned the Virginia State Police surrounding them.

"Put your hands up slowly, Leigh," he said from behind her, his voice steady.

"Keep your hands where we can see them and step out of the hotel room," the nearest officer demanded.

They complied.

"Hands on the wall," the order came from deeper in the group.

Hunter stepped beside her and placed his palms against the wall. She followed his lead, but her heart thundered in her chest. His gaze met hers, but he didn't make any promises or excuses.

When the police approached and started patting them down, Hunter asked, "What's this about, officer?"

No one said a word. When the officer grabbed her wrist and slapped a cuff on it, she winced at the burn of the metal. The cuffs weren't iron.

They were silver. Before she could struggle out of the cop's grip, they secured her other wrist behind her back.

Hunter's gaze met hers as they turned him around and slammed him against the wall.

Her breath locked in her chest at the pain radiating from her wrists. The crowd parted, and a visceral need to run gripped every muscle. The head of the national council, Ken Winters, stepped forward, but that's not what made her blood freeze in her veins. It was the look in his eyes as he stared at her, like he had horrifyingly painful plans for her.

His gaze landed on Hunter and a satisfied smirk surfaced. "I warned you." He pointed at Hunter.

"Fuck you," Hunter growled.

The exchange between the two men sparked a curiosity in Alessandra, but before she could ask questions, Winters gave the cops a nod and the closest officer hauled them into the back of a cruiser.

The officer who took the driver's seat in their cruiser wasn't human. He was a hybrid, and he glared in the rearview window.

"You have dodged us for the last time," he said with a drawl, his gaze locked on Hunter.

"Who do you think we are?" Hunter asked, his voice reasonable enough for the man to glance back.

"Fugitives."

Hunter laughed. "My father's a lawyer and he's going to have a field day with you." The deadpan glare he leveled made the driver shift. "Unlawful arrest. No one read us our rights, you just hauled us away with no explanation. Your men have the cuffs on so tightly the metal is cutting into my skin. I'm sure that could constitute police brutality."

"Shut your mouth. I can detect your scent."

"I took a shower, dipshit," he said.

The fact the cop wasn't human didn't help her unease. Hunter's little play acting, along with his strange interaction with Winters, made this much harder for her to deal with. All she could think about was the nightmare that had led to their night of passion. The certainty that he was being led to his death ate at her insides as much as the silver was burning through her wrists.

"I smell damned good," Hunter added, like he didn't understand what the driver was getting at.

"He didn't do anything," Alessandra said.

The cop glared back.

"He killed humans," he said.

"Stop talking, Leigh," Hunter said.

"They arrested us, Jake." Her voice rose. "They think we're someone else," she added, playing along with whatever game he was trying to play.

The cop's brow creased, and he reached for the radio. "Boss, are you sure these are the ones you're looking for?" he asked real softly.

"That's the killer we've been tracking. Bring them in and we will take care of them once and for all."

Hunter's eyes conveyed the same dread pummeling her muscles.

"Do you know why I'm wanted?" she asked, after he had put the radio back in place.

"You harbored a fugitive. A fugitive who killed for sport."

Now she was thoroughly confused, but she pressed on. "I did not kill for sport. I killed to survive."

"It doesn't matter."

"So, I just should have just let the belladonna they injected in me run its course? Kill me like they intended?" She didn't want to go down without a fight, and if her dream was any indication of reality, Hunter was going to be ripped to shreds by the council pack before they turned on her.

He glared in the mirror. "Yes. Killing humans is not tolerated for any reason."

"Even if the filthy pigs deserved it?" Alessandra said.

"Stop talking, Leigh." The anger flared in Hunter's voice, turning it into a feral growl. "It won't change a thing. This fucker's been paid off."

The cop's glare moved to the mirror and then back to the road. "You understand the price for taking a human life."

Alessandra's fear morphed, sending a dose of adrenaline through her entire form. If she didn't do something, they both would die. She hauled her knees to her chest, catapulting her feet into the back of the driver's seat with all the strength her alpha blood allowed. The impact threw the driver forward onto the steering wheel. A loud crack filled the car, and the driver remained slumped over the wheel.

The car sped up, and Hunter tackled her on the seat, driving her down with his shoulder. Screaming metal filled the small space, and the cruiser flipped. She had no idea how many times they hit the cage or the ceiling, but when the car finally came to rest, not one window remained.

"Hunter?" she whispered, her head still spinning enough that she wasn't sure if they were upright or not.

"Fuck," he whispered from under her.

Alessandra rolled off him, landing on the hard metal roof next to him.

"We need to get out of here," she said.

"No shit." His voice strained with pain.

"Are you okay?"

"No, but we need these cuffs off before I can tell just how fucked up I am."

Alessandra rolled towards the open window. Once she was on the ground, she curled into a ball and forced her hands under her butt. She managed to get her arms in front of her before she crawled to the front driver's side window.

Hot liquid dripped into her eye, stinging. The keys hung from the ignition and the cop's dead stare looked off towards the passenger side. His nose looked as if someone had pressed it inside his face. The impact with the steering wheel had killed him instantly.

She reached for the keys, pulling them out. It took her a minute to find the right one and once she did, her cuffs were easily unlocked. She crawled back to Hunter. He lay face down on the roof, his hands still locked behind his back. She unlocked his cuffs, but he didn't move.

"Hunter?" She rolled him over and gasped. The side of his face was covered in blood. She reached under his arms and hauled him out the window, falling back with his head in her lap. "Please wake up," she whispered. The panic created a flush through her, fueled by adrenaline. Even though she sensed life still present, she leaned over and put her ear to his chest. His heart pumped, but it wasn't strong like the beat that had filled her dreams last night.

Their only hope of escape was to shift and make a run for the woods, but she wasn't leaving without him. She scanned the ravine they'd ended up in and up the hill towards the road. No one peered over the edge. At least, not yet.

"Hunter, wake your ass up!" she growled low. She was aware of the dangers of shifting to the human body if it was broken, but in wolf form, they would heal faster. She covered his lips with hers, planting a kiss. "Wake up," she commanded.

He groaned under her, and his eyes flittered open. "You need to run," he said. "Keys are in my pocket. Go."

She laughed.

"I can't feel my legs," he said, meeting her gaze.

"Shift and run with me." Her heart squeezed in agony.

"I'm already dead, Leigh. You aren't. Please," he pleaded.

Tears blurred her vision as he fumbled in his pocket. He slid the keys into her hand. "Go."

"Jacob Blaez, shift your ass and run with me!" Her breath hitched in her chest.

"Run, before they get here. If I can smell them, so can you. Now go." His voice held the power of an alpha command and she backed away.

"Damn it, Jacob, I love you."

He stared into her eyes. "I love you, too, and if I'm not as bad off as I think I am—I'll find you. I promise."

She blinked the tears away and pressed her lips together to keep her chin from trembling.

"Go," he commanded.

Alessandra turned and placed the key ring between her teeth. In two strides, her large paws came into view, and she was flying down the ravine as fast as her wolf's legs would take her.

The freedom of the run usually gave her a rush, but this time, each bound away from Hunter squeezed her midsection tighter. She skidded to a halt at his scream of pain, but his command to go still rang in her ears.

By the time she slinked behind the row of hotel rooms, she was unsure what would greet her in the parking lot. Lifting her nose in the air, the lingering odor of humans remained. She needed the Jeep, and that clinched her decision. She shifted back to her human form and took the keys from her mouth. Barefoot and windblown, she stepped around the corner of the hotel into the nearly empty parking lot.

Hunter's Jeep still sat locked where they had left it. Beyond it sat a couple of empty sedans. Guessing she had a small window of opportunity, she trotted to the car, unlocked the door, and slid into the driver's seat. She checked the console and sighed in relief that the box of cash still remained.

Alessandra pulled out of the parking lot, turning south, just like Hunter had wanted, but she didn't get far. The pains in her stomach nearly doubled her over and her breath started catching in her throat. Sobs spilled, and she had to pull over to the side of the road.

She couldn't leave him to the council's mercy. She couldn't let him pay for her sins.

Alessandra turned the car around and headed towards the accident site.

Chapter 8

HUNTER STARED AFTER THE stunning gray wolf as she galloped away at a pace even a car wouldn't be able to keep up with. He wanted to be running alongside her, but with how broken his body was at the moment, he wasn't sure he'd ever walk again, never mind run.

A car skidded to a stop at the top of the ravine and the first of several faces peered over the side. When the head of the council joined the row of police, Hunter let out a low warning growl. He couldn't help the reaction. This man was the one his father had evidence against. This was the fucker who had killed his dad.

The old man hopped over the bent guardrail and slid down the ravine wall, coming to a stop inches from Hunter.

"Where is it?" he growled, as he hunched over to look in the car.

"Damned if I know," Hunter whispered. He meant for it to come out with some strength, but his was slowly seeping away. "Why don't you go crawl back into your hole?" he asked.

Ken Winters, the grand chairman of the werewolf council, sneered at him. He pointed his finger at Hunter and a sharp nail grew from the blunt tip. In a motion that belied his age, he jammed his fingernail into Hunter's shoulder.

The brittle pain caught him off guard, and he clamped his mouth as quickly as he could, but it wasn't fast enough to catch his initial cry of pain. He wouldn't let that happen again, especially with the master's sadistic smile beaming above him.

"I will find what your father gave you."

"Fuck you," Hunter said from between clenched teeth. He wasn't in any condition to fight back and he knew this line of questioning was going to get worse before he finally accepted death. The wolf in him bristled at the thought, unwilling to just lie down and die.

Winters crouched down next to him, twisting his finger, digging the dagger deeper into Hunter.

Hot agony gripped his shoulder, and he concentrated on drawing a breath through his nose instead of his tightly clamped lips.

"You seem fond of the girl. I'm sure once I have her, you'll sing a different tune," he said, after studying Hunter.

The dagger embedded in his shoulder retracted, providing temporary relief. He closed his eyes, ignoring the orders Winters barked at the men surrounding them. This was a walk in the park compared to what would come next. The council didn't care about their wolves. All they gave a damn about was power and wealth. And anyone who got in their way was trampled.

Alessandra did not get just how corrupt Winters was. But he knew only too well. His father paid the price when he attempted to expose the bastards for killing at will. Humans and werewolves alike. Sometimes the council wiped out entire communities just because they wouldn't conform to their rules.

Now, it looked like he would follow in his father's footsteps.

He closed his eyes. The proof that he had to bring these assholes down was buried under the money box right alongside his birth certificate. He wished he had shared it with Alessandra before the shit hit the fan, but he hadn't figured out who to send it to. There wasn't anyone who could challenge the council and win.

He finally opened his eyes to two of Winters' lackeys arguing over how to get him out of the ravine.

"I want him alive!" Winters yelled from the road.

Of course, the bastard wanted him alive. He wanted a spectacle, one that was sure to draw Alessandra from hiding. Hunter just hoped that she would heed his orders. The need to call her back had almost overwhelmed him, but if she had stayed, Winters would have everything he wanted.

The two men hauled him up the ravine and threw him into a truck bed. The impact drew a grunt from him. They splayed him out using silver shackles and left him staring at the bright sky. He didn't ask where they were taking him. He didn't care.

Each bump created a host of agonies through his body. He closed his eyes, willing either sleep or unconsciousness to come so he could attempt to heal. The silver ensnaring his wrists and ankles made either choice nearly impossible. Every now and then, Alessandra's scent drifted into his nostrils, like a promise of a dream, pulling him back into consciousness.

By the time the truck turned off the interstate, the sun had moved across the heavens and the deep blue sky of late afternoon greeted his exhausted gaze. Hours of torture seemed like child's play compared to the jolting bumps the side roads contained. Crunching sounds of gravel along with a thick canopy of trees made his heart race. Just by the heavy pine scent, he placed them in the mountains.

This was where the council carried out sentencing. He had heard rumors, and despite his injuries, the thought of being drowned in silver sent an involuntary shiver through him. His father had once told him that Winters had a trophy room for all those he'd sentenced to death. Screaming faces cast in silver lined the walls.

Hunter's throat closed, and he forced a breath into the tight space. If he panicked now, he might unwillingly give up Alessandra just to avoid that kind of death. The trees thinned until all he saw was the open sky and a variety of cranes. The truck came to a stop under one of the crane hooks.

Without a word, the driver got out, hooked the crane to something over Hunter's head, and gave a twirl of his index finger. An engine roared to life and chains rose, pulling a bar that they clasped Hunter to up into the air. Hunter glanced down to see his legs had a similar bar, and that one was attached to the truck. The crane didn't stop when he was fully extended and the pull in his abdomen yanked a cry of pain.

The driver made a cutting motion with his hand and the pressure abated, but didn't stop. Pain filled every inch of his abdomen. His arms ached, and he was glad he couldn't feel anything from his waist down. His brain hadn't had time to register his surroundings before the driver hopped up on the back of the truck and pulled out a hunting knife.

"Why are you doing this?" Hunter asked, and the man leveled a glare.

"Because beasts like you need to be put down," he said, and pulled Hunter's t-shirt away from his body before cutting the fabric off, leaving his chest and back exposed. He slid an ear-bud into Hunter's ear and stepped behind him.

A large clearing stretched before him. In the center of the clearing sat the werewolf council, lined up in a horseshoe around the focal point of the clearing—a giant vat filled with boiling silver. The metallic stench burned his nostrils, and he closed his eyes. An array of covered cages lined the outer edges of the woods, and Hunter wondered who else was being executed today.

"Ladies and gentlemen, we are gathered here to confirm sentencing, and carry out executions for the most heinous offenders of our species." Ken Winter's voice rose over the gathering crowd.

With a wave of his hand, the covers on the cages were pulled away.

The earpiece buzzed. "Look closely, Mr. Blaez. They are paying for your sins," Winters' voice whispered in his ears. "Tell me where the girl is and I will set them free."

Hunter's chest squeezed. Every member of their pack was behind bars, along with a few others he didn't recognize.

The loudspeaker crackled. "This pack, led by that man on the back of the truck, attacked a group of human campers without provocation, killing them just for the bloodlust thrill of it!"

"Bullshit," Hunter said, loud enough for the crowd to hear him.

Pain seared Hunter's back, followed by the crack of a whip. Heat traveled down his spine into the numb zone.

The man behind him chuckled. "You just keep your mouth shut or I'll put a gag on you."

Winters turned to the council. "Have you reviewed the cases put before you today?"

"Yes, sir," they said in unison.

"What say you?" he asked.

"Execution!"

There was no hesitation in any of the council members. Winters glanced at Hunter and an evil grin found the corners of his lips before he turned back to the crowd.

"They did nothing to deserve this fate!" Hunter cried, and received another lashing.

Winters gave a crisp nod to the executioner on the platform. The first criminal, thankfully not one of Hunter's pack, was dragged from the cages to the platform behind the vat. He struggled in the chains, but there was no use against the silver holding his arms behind him or his shackled feet. The crane hook lowered until the hooded executioner could drag it to the chains holding the poor bastard's feet.

"I promise; your pack will have just as slow a death as this man's." Winters' voice whispered in his earpiece.

A burning anger rippled through his muscles, and just because both Winters and the man behind him was a sadistic bastard, the shards of the whip ripped through his skin.

"I'm sure the stench of your blood will bring your little whore running. And just for the record, I will not kill her like the rest of these misfits. I'm going to chain her in a room with your silver coated remains, just so she remembers her place in the pack."

Hunter growled, and the chain above him pulled, yanking the air from his lungs. The struggling criminal rose into the air at the same time. Hunter watched in horror as the man was dunked headfirst into the boiling vat, his scream cut off almost as soon as it started. The crane stopped when the man's shoulders hit the surface, but his death throes continued.

Hunter could almost hear the screams below the surface as silver invaded all the orifices, burning as much as sulfuric acid. He shuddered. At least this death was quicker than lowering someone in feet first. That would be a slower death, one that would be wrapped in agony. Headfirst, there was perhaps two to three minutes of agony before that first inhalation of silver.

They splayed the next criminal out in the same form as Hunter. The bar attached to his hands hit the silver first and the moment the poor bastard's hands dipped below the surface, the choking screams began, along with sobbing pleas. Hunter swore to himself that he would not so much as whimper. He would not give the council the satisfaction of his screams.

Chapter 9

ALESSANDRA NEARLY RAN THE jeep into the opening behind the crowd watching the council. Instead, she shot down a smaller side path to the right that seemed to dwindle to nothing but brush. She parked next to a fallen tree and closed her eyes. The ride had taken forever, and her body ached from sitting in the same position for so long. Her bladder was near exploding and she jumped out of the car and squatted behind it, relieving herself.

Hunter had to have weapons she could use in the jeep and now that she was parked, she opened the back and searched through the trunk. Nothing beyond a crowbar was visible. She took a chance, lifting the carpet liner to the wheel well below.

Warmth flushed her skin at the crossbow lying in the well instead of a spare tire. She reached down and touched the arrow tips, yanking her hand away at the burn of silver. Jesus, she expected a hunting rifle or something. Not silver-tipped arrows. Where the hell had he gotten these?

Never mind where, when had he gotten them?

She pulled the quiver from under the crossbow and jammed the dozen arrows in before hauling it over her shoulder. The only other weapon she was aware of was the scalpel in the medical kit.

As she opened the door, the first scream caught her attention. She lifted her nose, catching scents in the light wind. She couldn't tell how many werewolves were in the clearing, but the scents on the wind made little sense. Her heart clanged into overdrive, creating the tingling sensation of urgency through her. The overwhelming need to get to that clearing gripped her. She made sure the quiver was secure and slung it over her head. The handle of the crossbow barely fit in her human mouth, but within a blink, her canine jaws had no issue carrying the bow.

With the wind in her favor, she opted for speed instead of stealth. She stopped just short of the woods line, horrified by the scene in the clearing. She transitioned back into human form and readied the crossbow with shaking hands.

They had stretched Hunter between two bars on the back of a truck. A man with a psychotic leer held a bloodied whip in his hand. But that wasn't what had her throat locked closed. It wasn't even the screaming man being slowly immersed in what had the aroma of boiling silver that had her heart racing.

It was the sight of her pack in the execution line that burned away any hint of fear, replacing it with an all-consuming anger. How could the council hold them responsible for what she did? What. The. Hell?

She moved toward the clearing, and Hunter's head turned in her direction. She swore he could see her, but he closed his eyes and tucked his chin in, like he was hiding from the horror in front of him. The whip cracked.

Alessandra had an arrow fitted to the crossbow before she finished her next breath. She drew it back, wondering if anyone would notice if she took that fucker out. She had close to fifty yards from where she squatted to where Hunter was chained.

The man on the execution track was still screaming, and all eyes were on that spectacle. If she miscalculated, the arrow could kill Hunter. It had been years since she shot a bow, but she didn't think she had lost her touch. She aimed, exhaled and depressed the trigger.

The whistle on the wind pulled Hunter's gaze back in her direction, but the screaming of the criminal had reached an earsplitting note that completely masked the clunk of the jerk in the back of the truck.

"Place is rigged."

Hunter's voice traveled to her ears and his tone carried both agony and anger. He glanced sideways toward the woods before refocusing on the gruesome death in front of him.

The screams stopped abruptly, but the body continued to struggle. Alessandra refused to think about what that meant. Soon, it was clear, as the youngest member of her pack was led to the executioner circle. Charity had been the one who had freed her from the rope tying her in the clearing.

"Winters, I swear if you do this, I'll see you dead before the moon rises tonight," Hunter growled from his perch. His voice sounded strong, but she had a deeper insight. He smelled like death, and her heart squeezed at the thought.

The head of the council laughed at him. "That will be a very neat trick, Mr. Blaez. You seem to have the same dementia that your father had just before we executed him."

Alessandra gasped. She thought his father had died in a hunting accident.

"They didn't do anything. I was the one who killed those kids," he said, and Alessandra almost stepped out of the woods.

She had already fitted another arrow into the bow, but she was unsure of where to aim this one.

"That is precisely why they are here. They did nothing to stop you and your mate."

"She was my alpha, not my mate," Hunter said, and then cried out.

The screech of metal grabbed her attention. The chain above Hunter creaked as it tried to pull tighter. His skin on his abdomen stretched thin, and she knew damned well where she had to aim. It would give away her position, but if she didn't, her nightmare of him being torn in half would come true.

She repositioned herself closer to the crowd where she could get a view of what held him to the truck bed. She climbed a tree to get a better vantage point, ignoring Charity's panicked pleas. With the ankle braces in view, she held her breath. When the girl's first scream shattered the afternoon, Alessandra let the arrow fly. Silver slammed against silver, and Hunter looked down. One ankle hung untethered.

The second arrow unclasped the other ankle bond, freeing both his feet. Yet they still dangled in place. Relief flooded his features, and he closed his eyes, hanging his head.

Her gaze jumped to the dying girl. They dipped her arms into the silver up to her elbows. The skin above the silver blackened at the burn. Her long hair touched the liquid and sparked an inferno that engulfed her head. Her screams pressed on her chest like a giant crushing her.

She strung the next arrow and let it fly. The silver tip pierced right through Charity's heart, ending her suffering in one motion. Chaos erupted. The crowd behind the council dispersed as if being near the council was dancing with death.

Winters pushed a button on the box he was holding. Hunter was yanked high into the air.

All the strength in her limbs gave out.

The crane turned until Hunter hung right over the center of the boiling pot of silver.

Her heart squeezed. She couldn't lose Hunter. Not now. Not after letting him in. She needed him by her side. She stared at the only man on this earth she was willing to die for and made a vow to herself. From this moment forward, they would be together, whether it was in life or in death. Alessandra reached for another arrow and strung it in the crossbow.

Winters barked orders.

Alessandra jumped to the next tree and climbed to a larger limb, one that gave her a greater view of the landscape. Guards, both in human and wolf form, ran towards where she stood. She had the advantage of being upwind and detected the scent of fear even from this distance.

Her muscles clenched with terror as one of the human guards raised a rifle. She aimed the arrow and pressed the trigger. He went down before he could find her in the scope.

She reached into the quiver behind her and her heart lurched. She only had one arrow left. With a trembling hand, she pulled it out and loaded it into the crossbow. Three concurrent snaps made her jump and nearly lose her balance. The empty quiver slid down her arm and fell before she could catch it. When it hit the ground, another metal snap sounded.

Howls of pain filled the meadow, and she scanned the landscape. Three wolves were trying to pull free from sharp teeth spring traps. Alessandra detected the scent of the blood flowing from each trapped leg. Those traps had been meant for her. A chill ran down her spine.

Hunter's lips formed the word run, but she couldn't leave him and her pack to die. Not for her sins.

The loudspeaker crackled, and Alessandra's gaze jumped towards Winters, the head of the werewolf council. He held a box with a red button over his head, his thumb inches from Hunter's demise. "Alessandra Tate, you are surrounded. Surrender or I will personally press the release button holding Hunter Blaez. I will give you ten seconds to comply."

Her heart pounded in her ears and she judged the distance between where she perched on the branch and where he hung over the vat. It was a distance she could cover in mere seconds if one of those traps didn't get her, but she wasn't sure she could get there in time to save him. Not with gravity pulling at him.

Between each number, Winters' lips moved, but the speaker didn't pick up his words. Winters announced the number five in the microphone, still looking up at Hunter with a sadistic smile.

Hunter bellowed an angry growl, and he glared at Winters with such violent intensity that Alessandra reacted.

She hopped to her feet and bolted down the length of the thick branch, using the bounce at the end like a diving board. Throwing herself in the air, she twisted enough to aim and pull the trigger of the crossbow before she released it from her grip. She didn't wait to see if she hit her target. Instead, she shifted, stretching out her front paws and aiming for one of the poor bastards in the traps.

She landed on the wolf closest to the clearing, using him as a springboard, landing a few paces shy of the pot. The chain holding Hunter to the crane released and her chest constricted, pushing the burn of adrenaline through her. He fell straight towards the vat, and she launched herself in the air.

The heat from the boiling silver singed the fur on her stomach, but it paled compared to the rush of terror racing through her bloodstream. She had one chance and when her mouth clamped down on the metal pole he was tied to, another burst of energy flowed through her, and she flung him towards the executioner's platform. He slid to a stop and her front paws hit the wood, but her back paws missed.

She let out a bark of surprise when her hind paws landed on the hot edge of the vat. With a surge of panicked strength, she pushed off with all the power in her hind legs and landed in a skid next to Hunter.

Before her heart had a chance to beat, she turned on the executioner. He stood with a silver sword in his grip, but it wasn't held in an attack position. It was pointed at the ground in disbelief. His wide eyes and opened mouth gape stared at something behind her. She turned towards the council, and understood his shocked expression.

Her last lunge for safety had tipped the vat over, drenching the entire council in silver. Some stragglers behind the council screamed in pain as silver flooded into the third row of chairs before cooling enough to halt.

Metal clanged against wood, and Alessandra's gaze snapped to the executioner. His gaze was now on her, but it transferred from shock to a kind of awe she wasn't sure she deserved.

"Let my pack go," she ordered, and then realized she had shifted back to human form.

He tossed her the keys hanging from his belt. And then the man dropped to his knee and bent his head in submission. Alessandra raised an eyebrow and turned her head to look at Hunter. He was staring at her with the same wide eyes the rest of her pack gazed at her with.

"What?" she asked, suddenly self-conscious. She wrapped her arms around herself, and that was when she understood. She looked down at what was left of the front of her dress. It was in burned tatters, revealing her creamy, unscathed skin. They had seen her naked and drenched in deer blood, so the sight of her flesh shouldn't be a big deal, and yet it was. Hunter's gaze was locked on something she couldn't see, and she pressed her breasts in and gasped.

The werewolf leader symbol had formed in the ash on her stomach. No wonder the place was bathed in silence. She had wiped out the entire werewolf council and now wore the symbol of a leader, a position she had no idea how to carry. Instead of focusing on what it meant, she crossed and kneeled next to Hunter, unlocking his cuffs.

He stared up at her but didn't move, except to rub the burn marks on his wrists. He winced and did a poor job of smiling. He still had the lingering scent of death on him, and she swallowed the lump in her throat.

"I still can't move my legs," he whispered.

She palmed his cheek and leaned down, pressing her lips to his in a gentle expression of everything swirling inside her. "You need rest to heal properly," she said when their lips parted.

His eyes moved to the sky behind her and after a moment, he nodded. "Yeah," he whispered, and his eyelids slid closed. Hunter's breath remained steady, and she glanced up at the crowd gathering around her.

"He needs help," she said. Her pack, newly freed from their cages, picked him up and carried him down the ladder. The only vehicle that still had working tires was the original truck they had tied him to. Alessandra had him laid out on the backseat with his head in her lap.

Nathan, one of the older pack members, climbed into the driver's seat and started the car. "Where do you want to go?"

"The nearest hospital. He needs stitches and we need to find out just how serious his back injury is." She met his gaze in the rearview mirror. "And it will give you time to talk about what's eating you," she added.

He pulled out and skirted around the silver puddle. "Thank you."

"For?"

"For freeing us. You didn't have to return."

"We had no idea that you were imprisoned. If we had known, we would have come sooner." She brushed the hair off Hunter's forehead. "He would have come sooner," she clarified.

"You wouldn't have?"

She kept her eyes averted. "One of you turned us in," she said.

"None of us said a thing, Ally."

Her gaze snapped up to his. "Then... how come they plastered our faces everywhere for what we did?"

He let out a sarcastic laugh. "I've been listening carefully to the council member conversations. They tried to get us to talk, but even sweet Charity didn't tell them what happened. As horrific as it was to watch, those beasts deserved what you and Hunter did."

"I still don't understand how they knew we killed humans." If the pack hadn't turned them in, why were they being held? It didn't make any sense. She kept running her fingers through Hunter's hair. It was as soothing to her as she imagined it was to him.

"The council sanctioned it. They grossly underestimated our pack. We were supposed to kill you in that field, and die ourselves."

The animal blood had been used to mask her scent long enough for the pack to bite her. Even so, the thought of them killing her wasn't anything she entertained, despite what Jeremy had said. "Well, they tried to hide my scent with the deer blood."

"Actually, they expected us to kill you because you were dying."

"What?" She wasn't sure she heard him right. "Why the hell would they think that?"

He chuckled. "I guess it's the norm in other packs. When one becomes too sick, the pack turns on them to thin the herd." He visibly shivered. "I guess that's what they were hoping for."

"What the hell kind of wolf pack does that?"

He shrugged. "Apparently, a lot of them."

"That's so fucked up," she muttered. She may have been as self-centered as Hunter indicated, but she would never intentionally hurt her pack, and Nathan obviously was of the same mind. The pack was her family, and she could never intentionally hurt them. She turned her attention to Nathan. "Why would they want the pack dead?"

Nathan's gaze dropped to Hunter and then returned to the road. "You need to ask Hunter about that when he wakes up."

Alessandra looked down at Hunter's unconscious form before glancing back at Nathan. "I'm sorry we didn't come sooner."

He handed her something from the front seat. She took the fabric and unfolded it. With a soft laugh, she slid the chambray work shirt over her shoulders, threading her arms into the sleeves and buttoning it up before the heat reached her cheeks.

"Thank you."

"You are welcome," he said.

Silence settled over the cab while he drove through the woods. The jostling of the truck pulled a grimace to Hunter's face, but he didn't wake. She let out a sigh of relief when they finally hit the blacktop.

Chapter 10

THE STEADY BEEP INFRINGED on his dream, and he went to roll, but couldn't move away from the sound. Hunter's eyelids flew open to the white floor tiles below him.

"Hold still, Mr. Blaez," a voice said.

He moved his gaze until white shoes came into view.

"Where am I?" he asked.

"The hospital. We had to fuse one of your vertebrae together and need you to remain still for another couple of days. You had significant injury to your spinal column, but with the traction you underwent prior to arriving at the hospital, and the fusion of your broken bone, we are hoping to reverse some of the damage to your spinal cord, but you must not resist the position we have you in, okay?

His eyes closed as it all came flooding back. The car accident, the clearing, everything. "Okay," he said, ignoring the reference to traction. That was actually an attempt to tear him in half, but if it somehow helped, he would not correct the nurse. Instead, he relaxed. "Is Leigh here?"

"Your girlfriend?" the nurse asked.

"Yes," he said, refraining from moving his head.

"She went to grab a bite to eat and to tell the rest of your friends how the operation went."

Coolness passed into his hand, burning through his blood, and he sucked air between his teeth.

"That should help you relax. I will be back in a little while to check on you." Her feet disappeared from view.

The burn altered, sending heat through every muscle, turning him into a giant mass of putty. His eyelids drooped. The soft patter of feet brought his fuzzy brain back to the moment instead of somewhere out in space.

Her scent filled his world. Warm cinnamon and spice, with a pinch of underlying power that was undeniable.

"Leigh," he whispered, intoxicated by her.

"Jake."

Her breath tickled his ear, sending cooling heat through him that tingled all the way to his toes. His eyes snapped wide. His toes tingled, and he jerked in the restraints.

"Easy, there." Her painted toes appeared, clad in flip-flops. Alessandra's hand caressed the back of his head. "You need to stay still for another twelve hours."

"My toes tingled."

Her hair came into view and then her beautiful face. A face he didn't think he'd ever see again; and he blinked back the sudden mist that blurred his vision.

"The only way to heal is to stay still, even if you're starting to get some feeling back. This puts the least pressure on your spine, so just chill, okay?" She put her drink on the floor and stretched out underneath him. The way her hair fanned out on the white tile stirred a need in his core and she smiled up at him. "You definitely can't do anything related to that," she whispered.

Hunter raised an eyebrow. "What's that?" he asked, toying with her.

She reached up and gently patted his cheek. "Were you aware your scent changes just a little whenever you're aroused?"

"Really?" Hunter had no idea. He was familiar with the fact that women had different pheromones when they were horny, but he never really detected a change in the male scent.

"Yes. It reminds me of salted caramel," she said.

He stared into her eyes. "Why didn't you run like I ordered you to?"

Her fingers slid away from his skin, and she sighed. "I couldn't let you take the fall for what I did. Besides, I saved your ass, so, no harm, no foul."

"You have no idea what Winters had planned. If you hadn't gotten lucky..." He couldn't finish the sentence. Winters had told him that his trophy room would be a fitting place for Alessandra, especially with Hunter's silver-cast body forever witnessing her suffering. He had promised that what those fraternity boys had done would be mild foreplay compared to what he and his pack would do to Alessandra. Winters' foul words still clouded his thoughts.

"He would have marched us all to our death," she said, thinking she was accurately finishing his sentence.

Hunter laughed. "Not all of us. The rest of the pack and I would have died in that field. But you, no, he wasn't going to kill you." His stomach turned sour at the thought, and he chose his next words carefully. "You would have served his pack."

Her head cocked for a minute and then her eyes widened as the color drained from her face. Hunter didn't break her gaze.

"He had some very graphic descriptions for me, between his announcements to the crowd," he added. The coil of anger burned in his stomach and he drew a slow breath, calming his tightening muscles.

"Let it go, Jake," she whispered. Some of the color returned to her cheeks. "We made it out alive."

Hunter nodded but didn't comment. He wasn't sure what kind of life he would have going forward, but he didn't want to lay that on her right now. That would have to wait until she wasn't lying on the floor looking up at him. That was more of a sit-on-the-side-of-the-bed type of conversation.

"Nathan said I needed to ask you why the council wanted our pack dead."

Hunter closed his eyes and pressed his lips together for a moment. "Because I wouldn't give Winters the evidence my father had against him." Silence filled the space, and he opened his eyes. "He warned me he'd tear down everything I cared about if I didn't do as he commanded." He wished he could reach out and caress her cheek. "I should have known he'd use you against me. Especially with the shit my dad had on him."

They stared at each other for a moment.

"Why didn't you give the evidence to authorities?"

Hunter laughed. "Because the bastard has greased palms all the way up to the White House, and the justice system is equally as corrupt. I had no idea who to give it to."

The shuffle of feet and a throat clearing pulled Alessandra's gaze from his to her right. Hunter couldn't see anything, but from the sudden tension in her jaw, he could tell it wasn't someone she wanted to see.

"Ms. Tate?" the voice inquired, and relief flooded Hunter. He didn't want to discuss this anymore.

Alessandra put her finger to her lips and Hunter grinned. He raised an eyebrow.

"Ms. Tate. I know you are in here."

Alessandra rolled her eyes and sighed.

"What, Hans?" she said without moving.

Hans? He mouthed at her, and she gave him a single shoulder shrug. The pop of knees pulled his gaze to the side, and an older gentleman peered under the bed.

"As I told you earlier, we need to sort out some... issues," Hans said.

"What items are you referring to?" Hunter asked.

The man's tiger-like eyes swiveled in his direction. "Council business," he nearly barked.

Hunter narrowed his eyes, glaring at the intruder.

"Jake *is* the council," Alessandra said, leveling an equally intimidating glare.

Hunter jolted in place as if his entire body had been plugged into a socket. His gaze bounced to Alessandra, and she gave him a small smile of condolence.

The man straightened out of his sight, and Alessandra sighed. "We'll talk later," she whispered, and slid out from under the bed.

He stared at the spot she had vacated, his mind circling around the conversation and her last statement. The medicine fogged his brain, and his vision blurred. He let the high take him into a sedated stupor.

Chapter 11

HANS BROUGHT ALESSANDRA TO Winters' old house where the local police had converged. Nathan stood next to the entrance, along with an officer, who was scribbling in a notebook as Nathan spoke.

For a second, Alessandra had the urge to flee. Her muscles burned with it, but she forced herself to cross the snow-covered lawn to the front door. Nathan gave her a quick forward tilt of his head, but there was no warmth in it.

"Nathan," she said as she approached. The officer closed his notebook and retreated, leaving Alessandra, Hans and Nathan alone.

"Ally," he replied, but even his tone was frosty. His gazed moved to behind her. "You didn't need to bring her here."

Alessandra cocked her head, but Nathan just gave her an almost imperceptible shake of his head.

"She is the head of the council. She deserves to know," Hans said from behind her.

"What the hell is going on?"

Nathan traded a glance with Hans and then met Alessandra's gaze. She couldn't read anything beyond his poker face. He didn't speak, just waved her inside the house. The house crawled with police. They lined the hallways, filled the office spaces studying files from open cabinets. But it wasn't the police or the rooms on the main floor that caught her attention.

The scent of death and decay made her nose wrinkle. She didn't want to see the source of that stink, but it seemed that was exactly where Nathan was leading her. As they approached the far end of the house, doors leading to what she could only surmise as hell leaned open on broken hinges.

"You don't have to go down there," Nathan said from behind her.

"What am I going to find?" she asked, numb from the deep-seated fear spreading through her. She turned and met his gaze.

Nathan inhaled before he licked his lips. "Ally," he started, and shifted his feet. His gaze dropped to the ground before moving to Hans and back.

"What—"

"—Your parents," Hans blurted.

The numbness encompassing her turned to a burning fire, and her feet moved faster than her mind. She skidded to a stop at the bottom of at least two stories of stairs. Her hand shot to her mouth at the display of silver-coated death posed for Winters' entertainment. Mounted heads covered the walls and figures littered the floor. In the middle of the room lay empty chains, but the videos the police were cataloging showed enough.

Hunter's earlier comment about servicing the pack wasn't exaggerated. His choice of words seemed tame compared to what was flowing on the screens. She shivered and rubbed the gooseflesh on her arms, trying to return the heat that had fled from her the moment she stepped into this hellish trophy display.

The silver coat preserving the dead did nothing to quell the decomposing flesh underneath. At least not for her. The humans in the room didn't seem to take notice of the vile stench, but perhaps they had been trained to ignore it.

She scanned a room almost the size of a football field. "Where?" she asked, when Nathan stepped next to her.

"They all have plaques," he said, with a tone laced in the same disgust accosting her. "Winters was a narcissistic sociopath."

Alessandra forced her feet to move through the cluster of statues, her eyes glued to the plaques near the bottom of every posed effigy, instead of the mask of pain and horror forever preserved in silver.

The men were all posed in some subservient manner, kneeling with their gaze forced towards the ground. Some women were in the same pose, but there were also more disturbing poses, ones that reminded her of the whore of Babylon, making their screams look like ecstasy instead of suffering. As she got closer to the center, a pattern appeared. The few male statues looking straight ahead from their kneeling position held expressions of righteous anger instead of pain, and they all faced a woman posed in a lewd position.

Her gaze caught the name Blaez on one of the righteous statues. Alessandra stopped and stared at the angry and pained face of Hunter's father. She had seen that expression before on Hunter's face the moment Winters appeared. Her heart dropped to her stomach. She was reluctant to turn, but she couldn't help it, and sure enough, a woman positioned in an X-rated pose held another plaque with the last name Blaez.

She closed her eyes and turned away. She didn't want to see the plaques labeled Tate. Not now, but when her eyes opened, her gaze fell on another set of silver statues that pulled her breath from her body.

Her mother and father kneeled with their foreheads touching. The sorrow and pain etched in their expressions created agony inside Alessandra. It was as if they were both alive when Winters coated them with silver. Her gaze moved to the screens showering the room with the sounds of abuse. Her throat closed and she couldn't draw a breath. Her mother had 'died' years ago. The insinuation of life in their statue pose broke something inside her. The primal pain formed a scream that transitioned to a howl as the shift took over. The haunting sound echoed off the concrete and silver.

All her father's over-protectiveness now made sense. Especially if her mother's death had actually been a disappearance. There seemed to be only one path for the missing of her kind, and it all led to this horrifying room.

Alessandra turned and ran without regard to her surroundings. Her powerful shoulders knocked over at least a dozen statues, and more than a few of the police officers she passed had pulled their guns at the sight of a giant wolf plowing towards them.

"Don't shoot!" Nathan and Hans yelled as they followed her on foot.

Some force beyond her control gripped her, and she ended up in Winters' sparse bedroom. With teeth and claw, she tore the bedding to pieces between her wailing howls of loss. With feathers and pieces of cloth spread from wall to wall, Alessandra shifted and fell to the ground, covering her face with her hands.

"Holy..." a voice behind her made her stiffen, and she glanced over her shoulder at the cop standing in the doorway with Nathan and Hans.

"What? You've never seen a shifter before?" Alessandra snapped and sniffled as she wiped her face with dusty hands.

"It's not that." He pointed. Within the frame of the bed lay ledgers, along with neatly stacked one hundred-dollar bills. There must have been at least fifty stacks visible.

Perhaps this was what the police were after. Winters' private stash, and who knows what those ledgers held. Alessandra climbed to her feet.

She didn't give a damn about the money.

She didn't give a damn about anything except Hunter right now.

She turned and walked out of the house of horrors.

Chapter 12

EVER SINCE SHE HAD been taken to deal with the council issues, Alessandra had been distant in his company. Hunter stared at her from his reclined position on the bed. The nurses had moved him out of the inverted position after another round of x-rays showed alignment in his vertebrae.

He hadn't had any sensations since that first tingle when Alessandra whispered in his ear. And the prognosis was still the same. According to the doctors, he would never walk again.

But that wasn't his greatest concern at the moment.

"Leigh?" he asked, and she turned her gaze from the world outside his window to him. The haunting look in her eyes left him hollow. The last time he saw that expression had been after they'd rescued her from that field. "What happened yesterday?"

Her eyes glossed over, and her lips pulled at the corners. The fast blinking didn't stop a tear from escaping, and his chest constricted. He couldn't fathom what had caused the heart-wrenching pain in her eyes.

She glanced at the ceiling before she met his gaze and crossed to the chair next to him. "I know what happened to your parents."

He inhaled. "You found the documents in the jeep?" he asked, still wondering what caused her to look like she had seen a ghost.

Her eyebrows shot up. "What documents?"

He blinked. His mind was still fuzzy from all the pain meds, but even with that disadvantage, he caught her surprise. "The proof that Winters was killing innocents. That's what he wanted me to give up. If you didn't find the papers, then how do you know what happened to my father?"

She cocked her head and took a deep breath. "They were a part of his trophy display."

Hunter's brain slowly processed the information. Rumors, along with Winters' taunting, gave him a clue of what the trophy room encompassed. While he knew Winters killed his father, the fact Alessandra had said 'they' sank in. "My mother was there?" he asked, still trying to wrap his mind around that. The papers he had proved Winters was a twisted serial killer, but he never connected the dots as to why his father was so hell-bent on bringing the man down.

"Jesus," he whispered. According to his father, his mother had died in a car crash. That was just before he had turned twelve. Just before his father moved them to the northeast and started investigating Winters. "Winters had her?"

Alessandra nodded and wetness pooled in the corner of her eyes. "And he had my parents."

All the air in his chest blew out with those words. He still couldn't wrap his mind around his mother being part of Winters' collection. He blinked as Alessandra's words sank in.

"Parents? Both of them?"

Alessandra's tears spilled over. "The way they were posed... I think my mom was alive when they died."

A chill ran through him. Her mother had died when she was a teenager. Thinking about the possibility that she might have been at Winter's mercy for more years than he cared to calculate left him shivering. Christ almighty.

"Winters might have posed them that way to screw with you," he said, hoping it sounded as logical to her as it did to him.

Her chin trembled.

Hunter patted the mattress next to him and she moved to the spot and into his waiting arms. His eyes burned with unshed tears, and his stomach cramped at the thought of his mother having to do all the vile things Winters had insinuated he was going to do to Alessandra. The impact of what Winters had done to everyone he cared about tightened his throat, but the shake of Alessandra's body against his kept his own emotions at bay.

"I'm so sorry. This is all my fault," he whispered in her ear. He brushed his lips against the edge of her cheek and she pulled away. Her tear-stained gaze met his.

"Why is it your fault?" she asked again, wiping the tears from her cheeks.

"If I had just given him the papers…"

"He still would have done all this. He was a sick fuck." Anger laced her voice. He would have still attempted to kill us just because you knew about his psychosis.

"Maybe. And maybe he would have paid me off and left us alone," Hunter said, owning part of the blame for all that happened.

Her brow smoothed, and she sighed. "I saw the malice in the way he looked at you. He never would have let you live." She sniffled and met his gaze.

He didn't disagree, but they might have had a few years of bliss before the gauntlet fell.

"Did the doctors say when you're walking out of here?" she asked.

His heart plummeted at the change of subject, and he took a deep breath. "Here's the thing," he started, and shifted, unsure of how to summarize his condition on the heels of such bad news. "I'm never going to walk again."

She blinked and leaned back, staring at him like she was waiting for the punch line. It took a few moments, and then sadness filtered into her irises, and he cursed himself for blurting it out so callously.

"Ever?" she finally asked.

He shook his head, pressing his lips together, trying to push off the memories of running with the pack, of running alongside her. That wasn't in the cards. And neither was having the alpha dote on him for the rest of his life.

"No. And I don't expect you to stick around," he said, forcing the words to come out steady, without the pain that crushed his insides.

Her gaze hardened, and her lips thinned. The bloom of red in her cheeks spread until it encompassed her nose. "I'm not leaving you," she said through clenched teeth. "How dare you even suggest that!"

"Ally," he started, and her fingers covered his mouth.

"No."

He pulled her hand away from his lips. "You've got your whole life ahead of you. You don't need to be saddled with a paraplegic werewolf in a wheelchair."

"You don't want me?" she asked, her voice as small as he felt.

Hunter closed his eyes. "What I want isn't part of this discussion. This is about what you need."

"I need you."

Hunter opened his eyes and met her gaze. "You do not get it. I can never run with the pack. I'm not going to be able to go for walks with you or dance with you. I'm going to be stuck in a goddamned wheelchair." His voice rose to a pitch he recognized as much as the tightening of all his muscles. Anger had finally burned to the surface. "I'll never be able to fuck like a normal man," he said through clenched teeth as everything blasted through.

He didn't know who he was angry with. Alessandra. Winters. His father. The doctors. Right now they all were on his shit list, and the news of so many dead didn't help.

"Why are you yelling?" Alessandra asked, with a voice so calm he wanted to scream. The hurt in her eyes just fanned the inferno further.

"Because I'm fucking paralyzed, and that royally screws up all of my plans. Why..." He stopped himself from asking her why she saved him. Even through his current state of fury, he was aware that if the tables had been turned, he would have done the same damned thing.

They studied each other in silence.

"I think you need some time alone."

Alessandra stood, and he grabbed her wrist, kicking himself for letting his aggravation cloud his thinking. "I'm not angry with you," he said, forcing his voice into a calm cadence that belied the tornado inside.

"Then why push me away?"

"Because you deserve better than this." He waved at his useless legs.

She cocked her head. "What are you afraid of?"

He narrowed his gaze. "Stop trying to psychoanalyze me."

Her lips tilted into a whisper of a smile. "Sucks when someone does that, doesn't it?"

"Fuck you, Leigh," he said, under his breath.

"Back at you, Jake," she replied and twisted her wrist from his grip. He expected her to turn and leave. Instead, she leaned in and pressed her lips to his.

His mind stalled when her tongue swiped his lips. The kiss turned sweet and sultry, melting his resolve. He didn't want to give her up, but he didn't see any other way for her to be happy.

"I don't really give a damn if you're sequestered to a wheelchair. I'm going to be there for you like you have been for me. And if you don't cut it out, I'll order you to do as I say," she said, after she pulled away with eyes full of hellfire.

"Order me?" His voice cracked.

"Yep. I'll pull the alpha card."

Her hands landed on her hips, and if he could have jumped to his feet and stared her down, he would have, but glaring from a bed was the only thing he could do. It was less than ideal and had nowhere near the same results. In fact, he was the first one to break eye contact. Hunter huffed in frustration.

"Where do you want to go when you get out of here?"

"I want to go home," he said. He wanted familiarity and comfort. Hell, he wanted his bed.

"Do you think our houses are still there?" she asked.

"I'm talking about our place in Maine. The one I bought outright, and we lived in for a little over two months with no interruptions?" He challenged her with his tone. He hadn't even thought of their hometown, nor had he thought about the pack at all. He just wanted a quiet setting with no complications.

"We'll have to actually get phone and internet service," she said.

He'd thought she'd put up some sort of argument and raised an eyebrow.

"Nathan's taking the lead with the pack," she said. "He knows I need to take care of you for a bit. Besides, I nominated you as the council lead."

Hunter leaned back into the pillow. "Why?"

"You are the most level-headed werewolf I know, and there's a lot of shit to sift through. There was no way I was taking that on without you by my side. Besides, you're the better leader, despite the spooky ash marks on my stomach."

"Did you just admit I'm a better alpha than you?" This time, his eyebrows rose all the way to his hairline.

"No one, not even my parents could give me an order I had to follow. No one. Until *you* ordered me to leave that ditch. So, maybe I am."

He chuckled under his breath. "Shit got crazy," he said.

"It certainly did." She settled back into the chair. "I'm ready to sleep through the rest of the winter," she added with a yawn.

He said nothing, just watched over her as she leaned her head back on the padding and closed her eyes. That familiar tingle settled over him and she opened a single eye before she closed it again, this time with a hint of a smile on her sweet lips.

Chapter 13

THE COLD MARCH WIND howled around the house and the fire crackled in the fireplace, sending warmth all the way over to where he sat on the couch. The internet was spotty again, and he slammed the laptop closed, setting it on the coffee table before he ran his hands through his hair.

The lights flickered, and Hunter glanced towards the kitchen. "How close is dinner?" he called and peered at the mountains of papers spread across the kitchen table. To say the council was a mess was an understatement. Winters had been cooking the books and skimming off the top for years, which explained his stash in his bedroom. So, not only was the prick a serial killer, but he was also a thief.

The committee had paid for the rest of his physical therapy down in Virginia, and sent him home with Alessandra, an architect, and what had to be some of the fastest builders on the planet. It had only taken them a month to renovate the first floor with a master suite, so he didn't have to navigate the stairs.

They also sent them with all the shit that needed sorting, from valid crimes that needed to be addressed, to the nitty-gritty requests that flooded in daily. He had only been home for two weeks and he was ready for a vacation. On top of that, the bitter cold had settled over central Maine, which made the Florida Keys sound better and better.

Alessandra came out of the kitchen with two plates and took a seat at the other end of the couch, handing him one like a sacrificial offering.

"We might be eating by firelight," Hunter said, taking the plate. The meatloaf weighed the china down and he took the offered silverware before setting his dinner on his lap desk. As if on cue, the lights flickered again.

Alessandra was quiet and focused on her food, which was unusual. She was normally the one to pull the conversation out of him, not the other way around. He studied her profile and the tension in her posture.

"What's wrong?" he asked around his first bite of the thick meat.

"Six months, today," she whispered.

His gaze flicked to the calendar, and his appetite vanished. Their life had taken a turn into hell six months ago. All at the bidding of Ken Winters. Hunter had uncovered all the documentation in emails and the money trail leading to Alessandra's rape while they had sequestered him in the hospital in Virginia. The sick fuck even had the video those monsters took inside the van. Hunter could only stomach a few minutes of the brutality, but the video, along with the evidence he supplied the newly formed council, absolved both Alessandra and him from what they did to those boys.

But that event didn't take away the nightmares; although they had evolved for both of them. Now the nights were filled with ripping flesh, silver, and other horrors he would rather not focus on.

He slid his plate onto the table, and dropped his lap-desk on the floor, before spreading his arms wide for her. He signaled with his head for her to come to him, and she crawled into his grasp. After all this time, she still shuddered when he wrapped his arms around her, but he understood it was because of this particular date and the unwanted memories, and he couldn't blame her one bit.

Hunter kissed her forehead, keeping silent because there were no words that would wipe out what she'd lived through. Only time would heal her wounds. Time and his infinite patience. She hadn't actually been in his arms since the night in the hotel, and the physical sensation of her body against his stirred something deep within him.

She inhaled. "Salted caramel," she said, and he shrugged in response. "I haven't caught that scent since the hospital."

"I'm sorry," he started, but she stopped him, planting a kiss that sizzled. Every muscle in his body tensed with the intensity, and his arms tightened around her. Her tongue explored his mouth, teasing at first, but it soon escalated into a burning need. He groaned under it.

The lights finally succumbed to the weather, flickering out, leaving them with only the fire casting shadows. She pulled away and straddled his lap as she stared into his eyes. "I honestly thought..."

Her gaze moved away from his, but he hooked her chin, forcing her to look at him. "I've been a little busy trying to figure things out."

"Including me?" she asked, her eyes wide with the fear he sensed radiating from her.

"No. You're the only thing that's right in my life at the moment." He cupped her cheek and the fear in her eyes abated, turning into a fiery storm of desire.

She blessed him with a beaming smile and then leaned in for another soul-searing kiss. Again, that tingle spread through his entire form, as if kissing her was a reprieve to the numbness. Her tongue twirled with his in a magnificent dance that sucked the air from his lungs. Her hands skimmed over his shoulders and before he had any awareness, her fingers had already unbuttoned his shirt. The sensation of her palms on his chest nearly drove him mad.

Alessandra pulled away from his lips, and trailed kisses over his cheek to his earlobe before her teeth nipped, creating another shock of tingles. He closed his eyes and leaned his head back, enjoying the sensations of her hands and mouth moving down his body. "When you touch me like this, I can almost feel tingling in my toes," he whispered and opened his eyes. "It happened in the hospital when you whispered in my ear, too."

She looked up from his chest. "Really?"

He met her gaze. "Yes. So, don't stop. I like that tingly feeling. It makes me think their diagnosis was wrong." He had studied the x-rays. He acknowledged that it was wishful thinking, but there was still a slight chance of the impossible, especially with the wolf's blood in him.

She ran her fingers down the center of his chest, down to the elastic waistband of his sweatpants. "How much of that theory do you want to test?"

It wasn't so much the words as the sultry tone of her voice that stalled his brain. His legs were a shadow of what they used to be, with almost two months of non-use, and that played with his confidence. She hadn't seen how much his lower half had wasted away. The desire that swept through him moments ago disappeared. It was his turn to look away.

"Jake?" she asked, pulling his attention back to her.

"I'm not sure what I can...do," he said, meeting her gaze. This level of vulnerability seemed unnatural to him. It was as if the tables had turned, and he was the one afraid to explore this attraction. "I mean, I know what I can do with my hands and mouth," he added, with a twist of a his lips as he wiggled his fingers. "But as far as anything else..." He shrugged.

"And if I said I wanted to make love to you?"

"I'd be flattered, and I'd wonder what you had been drinking in the kitchen," he answered, and his gaze moved to her hands, now gripping his pants. "But I'm not sure if I have the ability to follow through." Heat filled his cheeks, and he met her gaze.

"Then let's just view this as relationship experiment number two."

"What was number one?" he asked, stalling as a measure of panic bit at his skin.

"The hotel," she said, and pulled his pants clear to his ankles, freeing one foot and leaving the rest bundled around his other ankle. She took off her shirt and pants, leaving on only her sheer underwear.

The flames of desire returned, turning his heart into an aching throb that echoed through every cell. Her hands slowly slid up his legs. The sensation was lost on him, but even in the dim light he could see her progression, and when she dipped down and kissed the inside of his knee, he cursed the gods for not allowing him to feel this. She didn't turn away from the atrophy in his muscles, nor the non-response from his body. Instead, it just seemed to fuel her.

She moved her gaze to his. "Any tingling?" she asked.

He slowly shook his head.

She dragged her tongue from his knee to the middle of his thigh, and while his breath quickened at the visual, his legs didn't bother sending the right signals to his brain. He thought his mind would crack when she took the tip of his cock in her mouth. His wildest dream of having Alessandra Tate giving him head was happening, and he couldn't feel anything but a distant tingle.

She looked up at him. "Now?"

He lifted a single shoulder and licked his lips. "Maybe," he whispered with a voice like sandpaper.

"Well, somewhere there's a reaction," she chuckled, and her mouth covered the tip of his growing cock.

Hunter thanked the gods that something was working. They had told him it was a slim chance and to catalogue what triggered an erection if he was able to get one. Alessandra's mouth. Check. He'd keep that catalogued for a very long time. Her slow head bob sent another wave of tingles through him as did the hollowness in her cheeks as she sucked.

What he wouldn't give to feel her lips sliding up and down his shaft. His heartbeat picked up, and he gently ran his fingers through her hair. "Leigh," he whispered, and she pulled away, meeting his gaze. He cupped her cheeks and pulled her to his lips. He needed to experience her mouth, her breasts... her pussy. God, he wanted to taste her, but before she allowed his mouth to cover hers, she slid her underwear off and positioned herself over his hard shaft.

His gaze remained glued to the space between them as she guided his cock into the folds of her pussy. She moved down his shaft with a moan. Her eyelids were at half mast, her mouth opened in a sexy pout. She took his hands and placed them on her hips.

Her slow rock turned his breathing into something akin to a pant. The flush of her skin and the hardness of her nipples pulled a smile to his lips. She was enjoying herself. He slid his thumb to her clit, circling at the same speed her hips moved. Alessandra nearly purred and despite not being able to actually feel the sensations of her pussy milking him, the simple fact that Alessandra had given herself to him completely, especially on the anniversary of her attack, brought him closer to his own release.

He leaned forward and took her breast in his mouth, sucking the hard nub while he still massaged her clit. He moved to her mouth, capturing her tongue in a frantic dance. His entire form tingled as she rode him. Heat pooled in the center of his abdomen and then exploded, yanking a groan from his lips. She pulled away from his mouth, arching her body as she let out a howl that sent a shiver through him.

Her body shook with her release and finally her breathing slowed and she relaxed into him.

He stared at the ceiling as she nestled on his chest. "I think I came," he whispered, astonished by that mere fact. That was something the doctors were sure wouldn't happen.

Alessandra started to giggle. "I think you did, too."

He pushed her away from his chest. "I wasn't supposed to be able to do that," he said, and her giggles subsided a fraction.

"Well, you did. I clearly felt it."

He started laughing. There was only one other explanation, but he didn't smell urine, so it clearly was an orgasm. His toes were still tingling from the power of it, and he wrapped his arms around her, pulling her into a bear hug.

"I love you, Alessandra Tate," he said through his laughter.

"I love you, too, Jacob Blaez." She kissed the curve of his neck, and another rash of tingles flowed through him.

"Marry me?" he blurted. His eyes widened as much as hers at the sudden question, and then he dropped his forehead to her shoulder, cursing himself for such an awkward proposal. It certainly wasn't how he'd ever envisioned asking her. He had exchanged the idea of him kneeling in the center of a bunch of rose petals for hiding the ring in a dessert. Never had he imagined he'd just blurt out the question after sex. She deserved so much better. Jesus, he didn't even have her ring yet.

"Did you just ask me to marry you?" She pushed him away so he would have to look at her.

He glanced up at her with his cheeks on fire. "Yeah, well, it just kind of...," he stumbled.

She threw her arms around him and squealed. "Yes! Yes, I'll marry you!"

Stunned didn't begin to describe it, and when she pulled away, he asked, "Really?"

"Hell, yes."

"You realize that was the lamest proposal in this hemisphere, right?" He raised an eyebrow.

She laughed. "True..." She leaned in and kissed his nose. "Do you want a do-over?"

It only took a moment for him to think it over, and then he shook his head. "No. I got the answer I wanted. Besides, if I had to make it big and fancy, it might take years."

"I'm not waiting years to marry you," she said, and yanked on the collar of his shirt, pulling him to her lips.

As their tongues intertwined, his heart sang in response.

THE END

If you enjoyed WOLF MOON, please consider leaving a review!

About J.E. Taylor

J.E. Taylor is a USA Today bestselling author, a publisher, an editor, a manuscript formatter, a mother, a wife, a business analyst, and a Supernatural fangirl. Not necessarily in that order. She first sat down to seriously write in February of 2007 after her daughter asked:

"Mom, if you could do anything, what would you do?"

From that moment on, she hasn't looked back.

Besides being co-owner of Novel Concept Publishing, Ms. Taylor also moonlights as a Senior Editor of Allegory E-zine, an online venue for Science Fiction, Fantasy and Horror.

She lives in Connecticut with her husband and two children and during the summer months enjoys her weekends on the shore in southern Maine.

Visit her at www.jetaylor75.com and sign up for her newsletter for early previews of her upcoming books, release announcements, and special opportunities for free swag!

SHADES OF NIGHT

The Monster Defense Agency demands loyalty and prohibits inter-agency relationships. And once you become an agent, the only way out is in a body bag.

When Sarah Stone and Robby Young train together at the agency's academy, sparks fly. And when they are paired as partners, they must muzzle their attraction, or they will face a firing squad.

All their pent-up frustration sharpens them into finely tuned monster hunters. Their ability to neutralize entire nests of vampires becomes the stuff of legends.

But hunting vampires has its own risks. Especially when Sarah and Robby uncover duplicity and corruption at the highest echelon within the Monster Defense Agency.

With a bull's-eye on their backs from both the agency and the vampires they hunt, Sarah and Robby's only hope is to take down the Monster Defense Agency.

But two against an ancient organization that trains monster-killers and knows all their tricks is even harder than it sounds. It's going to take all their skill and intelligence to kill this beast.

And being caught is not an option.

Shades of Night delivers forbidden mates, cool magic, and a kick-ass heroine in this fast-paced urban fantasy series.

Books included in this special edition hardcover:

Young Blood – A Shades of Night Prequel

Wicked Heart – Shades of Night Book 1

Crooked Soul – Shades of Night Book 2

Tainted Mind – Shades of Night Book 3

PACK MAGIC

She's a hybrid alpha scorned by her pack, until he arrives.

Daughter of a tribrid and a flame-touched alpha werewolf, Erica Young's course in life should be set. Except no one wants a phoenix-werewolf with a taste for blood to be their alpha.

When the head of the werewolf council shows up with a possible candidate to take her place in the pack, sparks fly.

Logan Blaez, the prodigal son of the council head, is willing to challenge Erica for the role of alpha, even if that means a fight to the death. Until he lays eyes on her.

Now he wants to claim Erica as his mate and rule as her alpha.

Too bad Erica isn't willing to submit, or give up her birthright.

A FRACTURED FAIRY TALE
BOOKS 1-10

Little Red Riding Hood, Cinderella, Brave, Rapunzel, Frozen, Snow White, Sleeping Beauty, Aladdin, Beauty and the Beast and Peter Pan – all fairy tales you know and love, but twisted, fractured into something new.

Shifters and magic claw through the pages of these fractured fairy tales, giving you a thrilling take on an old tale.

Will the heroine survive whatever the evil villain has in store? Or will Love conquer all?

Grab your hard cover copy of A Fractured Fairy Tale – books 1-10 and find out!

A Fractured Fairy Tale books 1-10 includes

Red, Cinder, Brave, Tangled, Frozen, Snow, Spindle, Jasmine, Belle, Hook

SEASON OF THE DRAGON

Monsters, trust issues, betrayal, and a near death experience.

What else could go wrong?

The end of life as we knew it didn't come with a nuclear blast. It didn't come with the deadly impact of a hurdling asteroid. No. It came in a wave of illness that swept the world with fear, and in our quarantined silence, the monsters awoke.

Leviathans, serpent kings, and dragons came forth from the bowels of the Earth. The season of the dragon began with fire and fury and ended with a new world order. One in which these giant terrorists held all the power.

When Mikhail St. Clare betrays the monsters by saving me from death at their claws, I cannot trust the last remaining dragon shifter. Not when humankinds' survival is at stake, and he had a hand in our near extinction.

The only thing we seem to agree on is our desire to annihilate the leviathans and unseat the Serpent King. Our personal futures depend on ridding the earth of these murderous overlords.

We thought crossing the leviathan-patrolled city where every corner hides a hideous death was our most lethal hurdle. But building a bomb large enough to wipe out an entire species carries its own insane levels of danger.

One wrong move and we could destroy everyone living in New York instead.

THE FALLEN VALKYRIE DUET

A fallen Valkyrie. A Fae-Wraith hybrid.

Enemies become allies to survive a god's wrath.

Odin's Order to reap an innocent soul from Earth makes me question everything I have ever known as a Valkyrie. Protecting the innocent is our basis for existing, and now I must decide. Do I blindly follow his order?

If I don't, I will be just another casualty in Odin and Thor's destruction of the realms. Anyone who challenges their rule dies a very public death, regardless of their origins. And now they have enslaved Earth.

Reyfyre, a fae-wraith hybrid, and one of Asgard's enemies, has been hiding in this realm his entire life. When he finds me, he offers asylum as long as I help him kill Odin and Thor.

With everything they have done, how can I refuse?

When a bounty is placed on my head, we make the decision to leave Reyfyre's mountain sanctuary and head to New York to get lost in the city of millions. But the trek across the Canadian wilderness brings us face to face with hidden refugees, predators, and thieves.

There's no other option but to survive.

If we die, then there will be no one left to stop the callous gods before they destroy the only realm left.

But are we strong enough to take down a god?

If you like dark twists on Norse Mythology, you will love the Fallen Valkyrie duet.

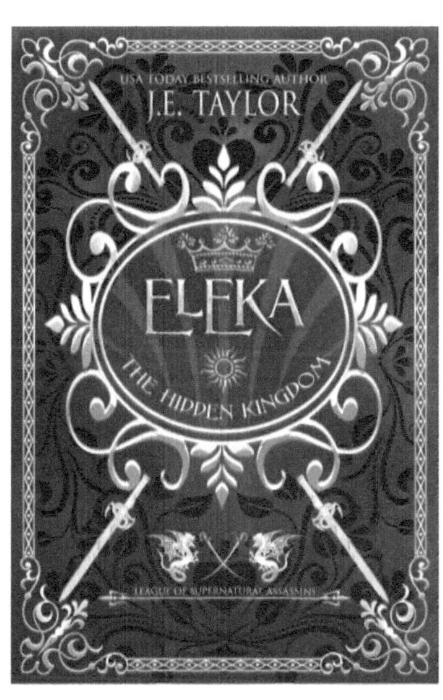

ELEKA: THE HIDDEN KINGDOM
LEAGUE OF SUPERNATURAL ASSASSINS

LEAGUE OF SUPERNATURAL ASSASSINS

When given a target, an assassin takes the shot ...... or suffers the consequences.

Genetically created as predators and raised to be assassins, they were trained to fight, obey orders, and kill. Those who didn't disappeared.

ELEKA THE HIDDEN KINGDOM

An assassin tasked with taking out a mythical fae king...

In a realm that doesn't exist...

Mya's mission is to get in, obtain the fae king's DNA, and get out.

It should be easy with her gifts, except when does anything ever go as planned?

When Mya doesn't return, the Director of the League of Supernatural Assassins sends an army of fae hybrid assassins to bring her back, alive or dead.

Avery's mission is to find Mya. If she fails, she faces certain death.

But confronting Mya may prove just as lethal.

ELEKA THE HIDDEN KINGDOM includes the following League of Supernatural Assassins titles: THE WITCH ASSASSIN and THE ELVREN ASSASSIN

SILENT NIGHT TRILOGY

Everyone thinks the Kringles only work in toy making. I'm not your normal Kringle and toymaking is definitely not in my blood.

Nope. I slay monsters.

But when Christmas rolls around, I protect Santa's sleigh.

Most of the time, we deal with a stray rogue monster or two on Christmas Eve. But this year is different. It seems the monsters have decided they want to play with Santa's reindeer and ring his bells.

If I don't put a stop to this madness, not only will Santa be their next meal, but children all over the world will wake to a Christmas that never was.

If they wake at all...

Silent Night Trilogy includes Joy, Silent Night, and Christmas Wish.

Find these titles and other fantasy and suspense titles on J.E. Taylor's website!

www.JETaylor75.com